C. J. FLOOD

SIMON AND SCHUSTER

This edition published 2014

First published in Great Britain in 2013 by Simon & Schuster UK Ltd
A CBS COMPANY

This paperback edition published 2013.

Infinite Sky and _Liquorice Cigarettes_ copyright © 2013 by Chelsey Flood

1 3 5 7 9 10 8 6 4 2

Simon & Schuster UK Ltd
1st Floor
222 Gray's Inn Road
London
WC1X 8HB

www.simonandschuster.co.uk

Simon & Schuster Australia, Sydney

Simon & Schuster India, New Delhi

A CIP catalogue copy for this book is available
from the British Library.

HB ISBN: 978-0-85707-803-2
PB ISBN: 978-1-47114-592-6
eBook ISBN: 978-0-85707-804-9

Cover lettering and map illustration © Frances Castle

Printed and bound in Great Britain
by CPI Group (UK) Ltd, Croydon, CR0 4YY

For Mum, Dad and Nanny.

In memory of Grandad.

PRAISE FOR *INFINITE SKY*

"an impressive and powerful debut" *The Telegraph*

"a heartbreaking coming-of-age novel about a summer that changes everything . . . [CJ Flood is] one to watch." *The Bookseller*

"a summer of secrets, new discoveries and daring defiance . . . a serious story that asks some brave questions." *We Love This Book*

"a beautifully written, poignant account of first love, so full of delightfully recognisable moments, it will have grown-ups welling up." *The Irish Times*

"loved by young adult journalists, C J Flood's debut novel is also a burgeoning hit among adult readers" *Stylist*

"*Infinite Sky* is beautiful. It made me cry . . ." Simmone Howell, author of *Notes from the Teenage Underground*

"*Infinite Sky* is terrific – moving, original and heartfelt. I loved it." Terence Blacker

"a beautiful, delicate debut." Nathan Filer, author of *The Shock of the Fall*

"sometimes a book comes along and fills a hole in your heart that you never knew existed . . . a beautiful book, one that I highly recommend!" *FlutteringButterflies.com*

"a beautiful book which will make you smile and break your heart... a real pleasure to read" *Overflowing Library*

"*Infinite Sky* kept me mesmerised from beginning to end . . . a spellbinding coming of age tale that throws heart break, anger, loyalty and love at the reader. This is a really outstanding debut. It is beautifully written, evocative and heart wrenching in places. CJ Flood is definitely an author to watch out for. I can't wait to read her next book." *Bookbabblers*

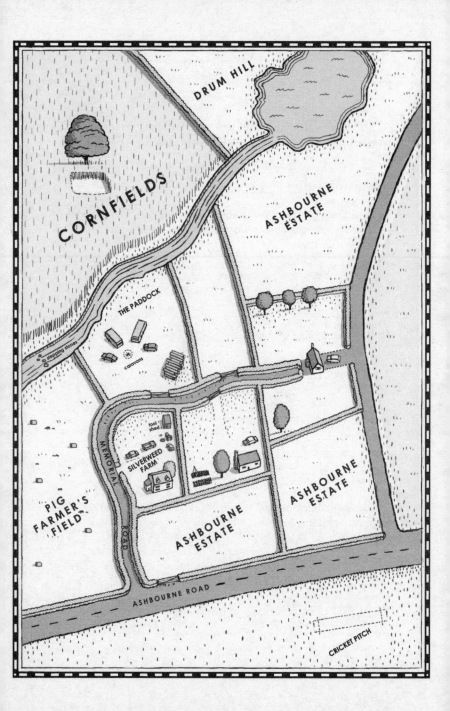

For most this amazing day, for the leaping greenly spirits of trees, and for the blue dream of sky and for everything which is natural, which is infinite, which is yes.

– E.E. Cummings

Prologue

You can't tell that the coffin holds the body of a boy.

He wasn't even sixteen, but his coffin's the same size as a man's would be.

It's not just that he was young, but because it was so sudden. No one should die the way he did: that's what the faces here say.

I think about him, in there, with all that space, and I want to stop them. I want to open the box and climb in with him. To wrap him up in a duvet. I can't bear the thought of him being cold.

And all the time the same question flails around my head, like a hawkmoth round a light-bulb: Is it possible to keep loving somebody when they kill someone you love?

One

It was three months after Mum left that the gypsies moved in. They set up camp in the paddock one Sunday night while we were asleep. My brother Sam was excited when he saw them.

'Gypos!' he shouted.

Sam used to have a gypsy in his class: Grace Fitzpatrick. She'd been famous at school because she could do as many things with her feet as with her hands. She could even write her name with them, which was funny because she couldn't read. Sam, who'd sat next to her in assembly, said she smelt like cat piss and fire smoke.

'They live off barbecues,' he told me as we watched from Dad's bedroom window.

I thought it sounded brilliant.

There was a caravan and a clapped-out car and, a few metres away, a fire with a pot hanging over it.

'Be bloody hundreds of 'em by the end of the day,' Dad said, emptying sawdust from his overall pockets onto the floor.

'They'll probably tarmac the field while we're asleep,' Sam said. 'Try and make you pay for it.'

Dad made a growling noise. 'Be a nightmare getting rid of them, that's for bloody sure.'

He left us leaning on the windowsill.

Sam made dents in the wood with his fingers while I wondered what Dad was going to do. This was exactly the sort of thing Mum would have sorted. She'd have been best friends with the gypsies by breakfast, had them falling over themselves to make her happy, even if that left them without a home.

'Look at all those dogs,' Sam said. 'Bet they fight them. Tie blades to their paws.'

I shook my head.

'Seen it on the telly,' he said.

'What, on kids' telly?'

He dug his elbow into me until I squirmed.

Two greyhounds bounded round the paddock and I tried to imagine them snarling at each other, blades flying, but it was ridiculous, and then the caravan door swung open, and a tiny black dog scurried out.

A woman appeared in the doorway. Tall and thin, with red hair falling over one shoulder, she looked beautiful. She lifted her arms above her head and stretched, revealing a stripe of tanned belly beneath her green vest. Behind her the white caravan seemed to sparkle.

'Prozzie,' Sam said.

The woman spun round suddenly, and a teenage boy in rolled-up jeans leaped from the caravan, laughing. He'd obviously startled her. The three dogs ran over to him, the tiny black one lagging behind, and he bent down to tussle with them. They licked at his bare chest.

Sam didn't have anything to say for a second. The boy looked about the same age as him. He was clearly the woman's son, tall and thin like her, but with lighter, ginger-blond hair that flicked out above his ears and curled on the back of his neck.

'Bet *he* don't go to school,' Sam said.

'Come on, Iris,' Dad called up the stairs. 'You're going to be late.'

'Aw, shame,' Sam said, because he was on study leave.

Still, I couldn't help staying a minute longer, watching as the red-haired woman filled a bucket with water from the pot above the fire and began scrubbing her steps.

Dad left the house at the same time as I did. With fists clenched, he headed towards the paddock.

*   *   *

I couldn't wait till the summer holidays. Everyone at school was getting on my nerves. *Especially* Matty. At registration, when I told her about the gypsies, she told me this story about her second cousin's boyfriend's brother: he was on his way to the newsagent's to buy a magazine when a gypsy girl burst out and cracked him over the head with a golf ball in a sock. For no reason. I told her we didn't have any girls, only a boy, and described the way his hair flicked out, but she curled her nostrils at me.

'Pikeys are gross, Iris,' she said. 'You'd get gonorrhoea.'

Matty was always name-checking STDs. She thought it made her look sophisticated.

At dinner time, we watched the boys play football.

'Your socks are odd,' Matty told me. 'Don't you care?'

'Not really.'

'Maybe you should.'

I took my shoes off and folded my socks down so their oddness was less obvious.

'That's your problem, Iris,' she sighed. 'You think that makes a difference.'

Before maths, next lesson, I nipped into the toilets and took them off.

Matty had moved to Derby from Guildford four years ago with frizzy black hair and too-big glasses which left red dents on her nose, but every new term she got prettier. Today her black frizz was tamed into long waves that she twisted round her little finger. Her glasses had shrivelled to contacts, and to make matters worse, her boobs had gone from a size nothing to a 32B in the last six months. As far as Matty was concerned, she was a fully mature woman.

'Remember, Iris,' she'd taken to saying to me, '*my* birthday's in September. *Really*, I'm in the year above you. *Really*, I'm a Year Ten.'

Every day, after school, I watched the gypsies. They hadn't listened when Dad told them they weren't welcome, and much to his annoyance were getting on with their lives. As well as the teenage boy, the dogs and the red-haired woman, there was a man, a baby and four little girls.

The boy spent a lot of time with his mum. He got in her way while she was cleaning, and made her laugh. Sometimes she grabbed him and ruffled his hair. They reminded me of how Mum and Sam used to be.

The gypsy boy was good to *his* sisters. They were all loads younger than him, but he still played hide and seek with them, and picked them up when they cried. I couldn't imagine him getting mad at them for something as silly as borrowing his socks.

In the evenings, they all sat around the fire, or on the grass nearby, until it was time to eat whatever their mum cooked in the pot, or their dad brought home in the car. Later on, when the mum had put the little ones to bed, the gypsy boy went to lie underneath the caravan by himself, and I felt as though I understood him completely.

Dad shouted if he caught me watching from his bedroom window.

'It's not a game, Iris,' he said, and so I kept my spying to when he was out.

One night, I left my curtains open so the sun could wake me. I wanted to see what the gypsies did first thing. It was well before six when I crept upstairs, past Dad sleeping with his head half under the pillow, to my usual perch on his armchair by the window. He didn't notice. Mum was the light sleeper – the snorer too. She used to make herself jump in the night.

Underneath the early white sky, the paddock was dotted with poppies, and fat wood pigeons in the tall poplars surrounding the yard called to each other. The boy got up first. He jumped down the caravan steps and did a lap of the field with the dogs. Occasionally, he stooped to pick up sticks, or tugged dead branches from the hedgerows.

By the entrance to the paddock was a huge pile of logs that Dad and Austin, his apprentice, had cut down over the months – a year's supply at least. Reaching it, the boy stopped. He glanced towards our house, and I ducked behind Mum's rose pincushion cactus. I peered round its spiky dome, which was flowering purple, and watched as he added a couple of long, slim branches to his pile.

Back at the camp, he knelt to build a fire. By the time the door to the caravan next opened, he was fanning the flames with a sheet of cardboard. His mum emerged carrying a stack of bowls, the baby wrapped to her back, and the boy changed position to direct the smoke away from them.

'Eye?' Dad lifted his head. 'That you?'

Dad called me Eye, as in ball. Sam had started it. Mum used to tell Dad off for joining in, back when they still talked to each other. 'She's named after the flower,' she'd say, but she didn't mind really. It was just something they did.

'What you doing?' Dad said now.

'Need some socks,' I said, pretending to rummage in the unsorted pile I'd been sitting on.

The plastic of Dad's alarm clock creaked as he looked at it. 'S'not even seven,' he groaned. 'Go back to bed.'

I watched the boy put on a rucksack, pat the baby's head, and walk to the far end of the field where the paddock dropped into the brook. He reappeared on the other side of the water, and then disappeared into the cornfields, and I wondered where he could be going.

*   *   *

8

I was sad to be leaving science for the summer. Biology was the best, not only because I got a break from Matty. I was in the top set, and she was in the bottom, and I paid extra special attention when Mrs Beever talked about the parenting traits of various birds. Apparently both male and female swans help build the nest, and if the mother dies (or drives off in a van to Tunisia) there's no need to spaz out and call the RSPB. The male swan is completely capable of raising his cygnets alone. I *almost* wished Matty was sitting next to me when I heard that.

All afternoon we bickered, but choosing sweets in the shop after school she still invited me to sleep over at hers that night. 'We can do a fashion show with my new clothes,' she said. 'Mum's making spag bol.'

'Doubt my dad'll let me,' I lied, putting ten fizzy cola bottles in a paper bag.

'He still being unusual?' she said, and I nodded, but the truth was I couldn't bear it round hers any more.

Her mum, Donna, asked questions with her best talk-to-me expression: Are you *okay*? And is your dad *okay*? And is everything *OKAY* at Silverweed Farm? The worst thing was that Matty didn't stop her. She just stood there expectantly, as if the two of them had become some kind of talk show mother/daughter duo, and I their favourite guest.

TWO

Saturday morning another caravan appeared. It was white, but its car was multicoloured: red boot, blue doors, silver body, and the passenger side mirror dangling off like a ripped ear. A man with an enormous chin got out, smoking. The gypsy boy was excited to see him. He went straight into his mum and dad's caravan, then came out with a pile of boxes, grinning. He spent the morning moving into the new caravan, shooing the little girls out from under his feet.

After he'd fed the dogs, the boy put on his rucksack. I wondered what was in it; maybe a book and a sketch pad and some pencils. I imagined him setting up quietly in a field somewhere to draw for the day. I imagined myself next to him, reading my book. It would be peaceful and relaxing and no one anywhere would argue.

The dogs followed him down to the brook, running into each other as they went. A minute later, the lot of them scrambled up the bank. They disappeared into the cornfields. His mum went inside to do the windows, while the little kids fought over some toy. The two men sat in the sunshine smoking and talking. There wasn't much point watching after the boy had gone.

I waited at the kitchen table for Sam to come down for breakfast. He used to get up early to get the paper for Mum – she couldn't bear anyone sleeping in. I was still hoping he would return to this habit; Dad liked to read the paper too.

At ten o'clock I gave up on Sam and went into the front garden with the dog. She still looked like a puppy, even though she was two. Dad had found her, whimpering, in one of the barns of a derelict farm he'd been clearing out. She was so small he'd brought her home in his pocket. She looked like a cross between a Springer Spaniel and a collie, and her ears were covered in long curly hair which Sam said made her look like me. She was the most difficult dog we'd ever had to train, which is why I'd named her Fiasco.

The sky was the colour of a sucked-out blue ice-pop as I hit the tennis ball with the coal shovel for Fiasco. It flew over the pick-up, past the stripped-down cars and abandoned chicken coop, to touch down behind the apple tree. Fiasco snatched it up as it bounced, and came back to drop it at my feet.

'Last one,' I told her, and toeing the froth-covered ball onto the shovel, I whacked it as hard as I could. Dog slobber landed on my face, and I ran into the kitchen to wash it off.

Silverweed Farm had always been messy, but two months without Mum and it was dirty too. The microwave was covered with paw prints where the cats jumped up, and there were dog biscuits on the floor by the washing machine. Furballs had rolled into the corners of the kitchen and living room. Underneath the plate cupboard I spotted a cat poo, curled up and drying out. I moved it with an old copy of the *Sun*, only breathing out of my mouth until it was safely in the bin.

Just after twelve o'clock, Sam emerged.

'Summer holidays!' I cheered, hitting a belter for Fiasco from the back door.

Sam filled the kettle, without answering, and I toned down the enthusiasm. I went to sit at the table.

'They've multiplied,' I told him.

He lifted one side of his top lip, the way he used to when he was pretending he'd hooked it with a fishing line.

His hair was getting long, like it always did in summer. It curled against the back of his neck, and sprang out all over his head. Matty was more in love with him than ever. She thought his long hair made him look like a film star.

'There's another caravan . . .' I said.

'You don't have to sound so excited,' he said. Water spilled from the spout as he put the kettle down. It hissed against the Aga. 'Dad's really pissed off.'

'I'm not excited,' I said, copying his monotone. I bit the inside of my cheek.

'Yeah, well. They're dirty bastards. Where d'you think they go to the toilet?'

I hadn't considered it. Their caravans? The bushes? The brook? My heel bounced under the table.

'Let's go and find out.'

'Find out what?' Sam said, rummaging around in the pantry.

'Where they *go*!'

'Jesus!' he said, sounding disgusted, and the blood rushed to my face. 'There's never anything in here! What am I supposed to eat?'

I hid my cheeks with my hands. 'Frosties?'

'Frosties? Again?' Sam yanked the box out of the pantry and took a handful. 'And they're soft,' he muttered to himself. 'Bet you didn't close the box properly.'

I laid my head against the wall.

'What were you saying?' he said, through a mouthful

of flakes. 'You want to find out where the gypos take their stinking shits? You serious?'

The way he looked at me made me shake my head. I tried to laugh.

'You're gross, Iris.'

I shook Frosties into a bowl, and shoved them into my mouth, not caring when I dripped milk on myself. Maybe I *was* gross, but why did he have to go on about it? His whole bedroom smelt like cheese and biscuits but I never said anything about that.

In the afternoon, Dad came home from wherever he'd been, looking stressed. He'd found out that he was allowed to evict the gypsies himself as long as he used no more than 'reasonable force', which he said as if it was a foreign food of which he was very suspicious.

'And what about all those blasted kids?' he said. 'How am I supposed to go about it? Bet that's the only reason they have the little bleeders.'

Sam laughed.

The police and the council could help, but they weren't in any rush, seeing as how the gypsies would just end up somewhere else illegal.

'So, what happens then?' I said, and he shook his head, tired suddenly.

'Exactly,' he said, rubbing at his beard. 'What happens?'

14

The beard was new. I couldn't get used to it. His chin had a cleft, like the tiniest bum. I missed seeing it.

His plan was to go down there and act as if he was giving them the chance to leave before things got messy.

Sam scoffed.

'What?' Dad snapped.

'D'you *really* think that's gonna work?'

'I really think you should shut your face.'

Sam stared at Dad for a few seconds then slouched out of the kitchen.

Dad watched him go. '*Blasted* boy.'

Upstairs, Sam's bedroom door slammed.

A few weeks ago, a letter had come from Sam's form tutor. Stapled to it was a receipt for a pair of football boots that Sam swore he hadn't thrown onto the swimming pool roof. He'd only even been in school to take his Art exam.

I'd snuck a look at the letter when Dad was making tea. *I'm concerned about the shift in Samuel's behaviour*, Mr Starkey had written. *Has anything changed at home?*

Ha.

It wasn't the first time Sam had been in trouble. Or the worst time. A few months earlier, just before he left for study leave, Dad had been called in to see Sam's Head of Year, Miss Ryan, because apparently Sam had started a fight with Benjy. *His best friend.* The two of them had been sent home, and Sam had been told not to take his place at Sixth Form for granted. I couldn't believe it. He'd always been so good till now.

Benjy had been Sam's best friend since they were babies. Benjy's mum, Tess, and our mum had pulled their beds together in the maternity ward. They'd made each other godmothers! And then Sam had split Benjy's lip.

Dad still hadn't forgiven him. He swore under his breath, and walked out the kitchen. He was going to confront the gypsies, I could tell.

I ran upstairs to watch. Sam came out his room to see what was going on. He was excited in spite of himself, and I smiled at him. His mood changes were ridiculous.

'Best seat in the house.' He grinned, bringing the dimple out in his left cheek. He jostled me out of Dad's armchair. I let him win, propping myself on the arm instead.

We watched Dad walk across the yard, with Fiasco beside him, tail wagging. The sun was high above their heads. Around the fire, the mum, dad and the bloke with the enormous chin were talking. The men's faces looked red and windblown like Dad's, and I thought they must work outside too.

The four little kids sat nearby in the overgrown grass, trying to hit each other's hands in a game of Slaps. They looked mucky and wild and I wanted to be out there with them. There was no sign of the boy or the dogs.

Sometimes, at the weekend, they stayed away all day. I opened the window, but the air outside was so hot it didn't make any difference.

Seeing Dad, the two gypsy men stood. The red-haired woman walked away, towards the brook. She held her hands out behind her and the four little ones followed, catching at her fingers.

'They're scared,' Sam said, and I couldn't quite tell if he was being sarcastic.

Dad was only metres away now.

'If they try anything, I'll leg it down there.'

I laughed.

'You think I wouldn't?'

'I think you *shouldn't*. They'd kill you!'

He glared at me, angry again suddenly.

'They're not going to fight anyway. Look, they're talking,' I said.

Sam bunched his hands into fists, as if he were ready for action, and I thought how sometimes being a boy made you act like a moron.

The gypsy dad folded his arms while our dad talked, making his broad shoulders swell. The man had a big belly and, standing with his chest out, his body pulled at his checked shirt. I wanted Dad to come inside.

'D'you think they'll listen?' I asked.

Sam blew air through his teeth in a kind of laugh. 'Do *you*?'

17

The gypsy dad was talking now. He'd relaxed his arms at his sides, as if flaunting his muscles for a few seconds was enough. He met Dad's eye and shrugged, and the bloke with the chin did the same beside him.

Dad held his hands out, and I could imagine him saying, all abrupt, 'Well. I gave you the chance.'

Walking back, Dad's face was dark as he looked at the ground. His mouth moved as he muttered to himself. Seeing us, he jabbed his finger at the air.

We ran downstairs.

Fiasco entered the house first, belting into the kitchen, mouth open in a grin.

'Bastards!' Dad said.

'What happened?' Sam and I asked together.

Dad picked the phone up and dialled.

The engaged tone throbbed out of the receiver.

I sat next to Sam on the bench by the table, while Dad flicked through the first pages of the phone book. He dialled again then slammed the phone down.

'Jesus, Iris!' he burst out. 'Can you *pack* that in?'

'What?'

'That *bloody* foot.'

I flattened my heel to the floor.

'Haven't you got owt to do?' he asked us.

Sam said he was going out, and I waited for Dad to

remind him he was grounded, but he only said, 'Well? What you waiting for?'

Sam dodged out the house happily.

For the rest of the afternoon I lay in bed, reading Dad's book about dragonflies and drawing pictures: slashed greyhounds with bladed paws, and caravans so full of people that limbs shattered through windows. I didn't see what the big deal was: the paddock wasn't being used, not really, except for the occasional dropping off or collecting of logs. So what?

Dad knocked a couple of times, making sure I hadn't died on his watch. That wouldn't exactly help prove to Mum that he knew how to look after us. Even when he called me, I didn't answer. I wanted him to feel bad. All he ever did was snap at me. He never did the shopping. We hadn't been for a big walk in weeks.

He left a jacket potato with melted cheese and fried onions in the Aga for me, and I sneaked out to eat it when the house was quiet. I fell asleep early and dreamed of being attacked by a stranger with a golf ball in a sock.

Monday night, Mum rang as usual and, as usual, Sam and Dad were nowhere to be seen. This time at least, I had something to say. I told her about the gypsies, and Sam's and Dad's reactions, and the stories I'd heard at

19

school, and it was the longest conversation we'd had since she left.

'They just want to be free, Iris,' she said.

'I know,' I said, even though it hadn't occurred to me.

When I'd finished, she told me that the Transit was holding up well, that she'd sent us a present each, and that she was halfway around the Mediterranean coast. The water was clearer than in Kos, she said; Sam and I would love it.

'One day we'll do it together,' she said, and I made some vague kind of noise because I could just imagine how Dad would feel about that, left behind at Silverweed Farm.

'Be careful, won't you?' she said, when we were saying goodbye. 'Give them a chance, but be careful too.'

'Course,' I said, but I wasn't listening. I was too excited.

I didn't need Sam to formulate a plan, and I didn't have to do what anyone told me. I was free, and tomorrow I would watch to see if the boy took his rucksack and the dogs across the brook again.

If he did, I would follow him.

Three

I planned to head straight down to the paddock – no indoor spying preliminaries; I couldn't risk waking Dad again – then I'd creep through the pig farmer's land adjacent to ours and watch the gypsies from there. If the boy headed off in the same direction as usual, I could dash across the stepping stones me and Sam had put down in the spring, and get on his tail.

I was shiny and full of myself as I pulled on yesterday's clothes. Mum's running shorts needed washing, but I couldn't face it. I was superstitious about cleaning her away for good. A fat Fiasco-print pawed the left bum cheek, and an orange stain patterned the white drawstring. I sniffed it. Beans. Matty would not approve. Climbing over the pig farmer's gate, I wondered what dry-cleaning actually meant, and if it was something I should consider.

The pig farm was separated from the paddock by a willow- and alder-lined ditch, which I crawled along until the caravans came into view. On the way, I bumped into our cat, Maud. Prowling through the grass with her nose to the ground and shoulder blades sliding under ginger fur, she looked wild and dangerous, and I wondered what was about to die in her claws. I copied her movements.

The gypsies' voices travelled from the caravans, and it was funny to hear them, like hearing your fridge magnet speak: something you hadn't considered. The mum was high-pitched and talked constantly as she rinsed plates in a basin, though I couldn't make out a word. The dad was silent. Hunched over on a white plastic patio chair, he laced his work boots. I couldn't see the boy yet. He must still be in inside. He never left earlier than this.

As I drew in, I realised the woman was singing. Her voice was soft and sweet, and I could see the way her hair changed from dark red at the roots to ginger at the ends, and that she was younger than I first thought – younger even than Mum. Green eyeliner surrounded her eyes, which were big and turned up at the outsides, and silver glittered on her ankle as she walked barefoot to empty suds from the washing-up bowl into a patch of nettles by the brook. She wore a long pale denim skirt with a V cut out the front so you could see her thighs, and even though I didn't recognise her song I could tell a lot of the notes were off.

The baby on her back started crying, and she stopped what she was doing and sang louder, swivelling from side to side, reaching with one hand to pat the baby's bum. The man didn't seem to notice them, just kept lacing his boots. I was metres away now, separated only by the ditch and the tall alder I hid behind. Its trunk was straight and draped with moss, and cones lay all around like tiny keeled-over dormice. The ground was soft, and I decided it didn't matter if the boy had already gone; I would watch the rest of them instead. I lay down in the long grass and peered around the tree trunk.

'Freeze,' a voice said, very close behind me.

I felt something cool and flat and heavy on my back.

'Get *off*,' I hissed, trying to roll out from under it.

The foot stepped down, and I turned around to see its owner.

The gypsy boy.

I stood up, brushing off dried blades of grass and a couple of ants. He was nearly half a foot taller than me, and on closer inspection maybe not quite so old as my brother. His jeans were faded and rolled up to below the knee, and he wore flip-flops rather than trainers, unlike the boys at school. He pulled my arm, leading me towards Silverweed.

'What you doing? *Get* off me!'

'Don't want me da to see,' he said. His voice was soft and husky and he spoke much faster than I'd imagined. He had an Irish lilt, but not like I'd heard before. I breathed in, but couldn't detect cat piss, just wood smoke.

'Well, don't go that way,' I said. 'My dad'll kill me and all.'

I dropped cross-legged to the ground, and he did the same. Cow parsley nodded above our heads.

'Not allowed to mix with the likes of us, I'm sure . . .'

I curled my lip at him, the way Sam did to me lately. '*You're* the one hiding.'

'Oh aye, we know what your da thinks of us . . .'

I lay back, embarrassed. It was nothing to do with me.

Maud caught up then. No sign of the maiming and murdering she'd been attempting. She purred and rubbed her head against me, then him. *No loyalty whatsoever.* He petted her, digging his fingers in behind her ears, and she closed her eyes.

'So?' he said. 'What were you doing?'

I stared at Maud, who purred loudly, and wondered how much to tell.

'Your da send you?'

That made me laugh. 'I was going to follow you,' I admitted. 'Wanted to see where you went.'

24

'How d'you know I go anywhere?' he said, and there was the slightest hint of his being impressed, so I looked blank, holding on to my mystery, but then he laughed, and told me he'd been spying on me too. Amazed by his openness, I asked him straight out.

'So? Where d'you go then?'

'I'll show you, if you want,' he said, and I looked indifferent, but butterflies were hatching in my stomach.

Still cautious of our dads, we army-crawled the length of the ditch, away from Silverweed, past the caravans, to where the pig farmer's land dipped to meet the brook. Brambles and nettles grew thicker as we approached, and as the grass turned to silt and pebbles, we no longer had to be careful.

'Didn't realise these were here,' the boy said, jumping across the stepping stones at the end of the pig farmer's field. 'I've been getting soaked.'

I didn't respond. I was remembering Mum standing here in March. It was the first warm day of the year, and we were showing her what we'd built. Walking across, she'd caught her shoe and fallen in. When Sam laughed, she pulled him in with her. I'd jumped in myself, not wanting to be the odd one out, and we'd sat in the freezing cold brook watching the waterboatmen paddling over the surface, trying to catch the bull fish we knew hid under the rocks.

The boy held his hand out to me from the Ashbourne side of the stepping stones, and he was standing precisely where she had; smiling, wringing the water from her long dark blonde hair.

'What's your name anyways?' the boy asked.

'Iris.'

I left his hand to dangle as I landed with a squelch on the wet bank.

'Trick.'

I waited, confused.

'My *name's* Trick. Too many Paddys at the old camp.'

We climbed the bank, stepping over convolvulus and ferns and the garbled roots of an ancient oak to the boundary of the Ashbourne Estate, which was a mixture of farmland and National Trust. Two rows of barbed wire surrounded a maize field that stretched on for miles.

Trick held the top wire to make it easier for me to climb through.

'Wait,' he said. 'Your hair's caught.'

I yanked my head, leaving a dark brown curl of hair trapped inside the metal knot.

'Christ,' he winced. 'Did that not hurt?'

I shook my head, blinking the tears from my eyes when he wasn't looking. I held the wire for him, and close up, as he ducked under my hand, I saw the faintest spattering of freckles on his nose, which was tanned like

26

the rest of him, and that his eyelashes were longer than any girl's. When he blinked, white-blond flashed at their tips.

'How far is it?' I asked, but he'd already started running uphill through the crop.

Long, thin strands of maize flowers waved in the breeze above our heads, and heavy green leaves whipped my face as I ran. We were completely hidden, and I wondered what he was going to show me: a nest maybe – something impressive like a kestrel or a buzzard – or a litter of feral kittens, but when we got there it was nothing like that. Really it was nothing at all. And that's why it was brilliant.

At the top of the hill, beside a lonely oak, Trick had beaten out a room in the corn. Narrow pathways led from either end, one to the brook and the paddock, where we'd come from, and the other – if you kept going for a mile or so – to Markeaton Park and the cemetery, and the ceramics shop over that way. The corn was so tall the pathways felt like corridors.

He threw himself down, and grinned up at me.

I grinned back, taking a patch for my own. The trampled stalks made a bumpy but comfortable bed. A few ripe corn on the cobs were piled in one corner. The rough grass scratched through my T-shirt and made my skin itch, but I didn't care. I half closed my eyes so that sunlight caught and glittered between my lashes.

The sky was blue and infinite.

Somewhere above us a skylark trilled, and a sweet, dry scent rose from the crop. Everywhere you looked fat little spiders ran in and out of the deep cracks in the earth, rearranging themselves like kids in a game of Sardines. I asked Trick how old he was, and he told me to guess.

The sun had turned his thick hair blond at the ends, and he wore it long and to one side, so that every now and then he had to twitch it out of his eyes, which were strange because the pupil of his right eye bled black into his iris. It made him look odd and quizzical, like he was considering some private thing that he wasn't sure whether or not to tell you.

'Fourteen,' I decided.

'Fifteen in September,' he said, as though it were a correction.

'So fourteen, then,' I repeated.

'And you're . . .' He dragged the last word out, scrutinising me, and I worried that he would mention the bean juice, or that my ladies shorts were tied on, or that my hair was matted on the side from fidgeting in the night, but he just looked at my face, from eyes to nose to mouth, and up again.

'Thirteen,' he said, 'no doubt about it,' and he settled back, letting his palms make a pillow for his head.

I would be fourteen next month, but it would be babyish to point that out now. At least he hadn't said twelve. Whenever anyone guessed Matty's age they *always* said older. Once a boy at the rec guessed sixteen, but he probably just wanted to kiss her. I was too small and flat-chested to be in my teens. And for anybody to want to kiss me.

'Your brother's older,' he said. 'Fifteen?'

I nodded. He was good at this.

'Older than me, then,' he said, as if it had been puzzling him for a while.

I asked about his sisters, and he said they were just babies, not worth bothering with, and he pronounced baby to rhyme with tabby, but I noticed that his words didn't match his voice, and I remembered seeing him on the caravan steps, leaning over to show them something cupped in his hands.

'I'd *love* to have a little sister,' I said, instantly embarrassed by the feeling in my voice.

'I always wanted a younger brother,' he said. 'People'd call us the Delaney boys. All the girls'd want to double-date us.'

He spoke so fast I was sure I'd miss what he said, but if I waited a second the words caught up with me.

Trick turned to lean on one elbow, facing me, and I copied him. Our bodies made a V.

I asked what it was like living in a caravan, and he said pretty much like living in a house except that you moved all the time, and there's no privacy, and I laughed and said, so not much like a house at all then.

'Me mammy's desperate for one,' he said. 'She loves the idea of it, unpacked forever!'

I remembered my mum, packing her things in boxes and taking them to Oxfam. I'd heard her talking to Tess. She didn't want to sit in the house drinking a bottle of wine by herself every night, she said. When you want things to change, you have to do something different. This is certainly different, Tess had said.

Trick was telling me how his da said he would settle when he was in his grave, and how he felt just the same. As soon as he was old enough he was going to get his own trailer and go all around the world.

'Just me and me wife,' he said. 'No kids or dogs or nothing like that.'

He pronounced that like *dat*.

'It's all right now my uncle's here, I'm in with him, but before that . . . The noise!'

He breathed out through his mouth to emphasise his point, and I remembered him lying under the caravan those first nights I'd watched him.

He talked so much I could hardly keep up. He told me about the old camp, where they'd pulled in next to his uncle, a different one, and had a great time until the land was sold for redevelopment.

'We ended up on the A52,' he said. 'Imagine putting that on a letter!'

I examined the tiny blue forget-me-nots which grew in bunches between the rows of corn. I couldn't imagine it at all.

I thought about Sam saying gypsies couldn't read, and I wanted to ask Trick about it. I wanted to ask how he got to school if he was living on the A52, but maybe it was a well-known fact that gypsies didn't go. But then, what about Grace Fitzpatrick?

As the sun climbed higher we grew slow and lazy like wasps trapped in a jar. He seemed to have talked himself out, for a while at least, and I was too hot to worry about thinking of things to say. Sweat trickled down the backs of my knees. I changed position occasionally, uncomfortable in the heat, but Trick lay still as a reptile. He basked. His skin seemed to glow in the sun, like it would never get burned.

I looked at the way his eyes moved underneath his eyelids and wished I was brave enough to ask him more questions.

A cabbage white flew into our hideout, and I watched it flutter on the breeze. I remembered how his mum had looked this morning.

'Your mum's really pretty,' I said. 'I was listening to her sing before you jumped on my back.'

He laughed. 'She's tone deaf. Drives me da mad.'

I thought of Mum practising her guitar, and how Sam would sing along with her. She tried to teach us harmonies, but I could never get it right in time. I got left behind.

The butterfly settled on a leaf. It blinked its wings, showing us the black eyes there, then took off.

'Haven't seen your mum yet,' he said.

'She doesn't go out much.'

I smoothed my hands across the thick, battered stems on the ground between us. He did the same.

'Actually. She's out all the time. As in, she doesn't live with us any more.'

I waited, but he didn't put on a fake voice, or gasp, or give me his opinion, and so I told him how she'd left for Beni Khiar with hardly anything packed into a blue Ford Transit van that she'd spent weeks fitting with a bed and storage space and a tiny gas stove.

'It's in Tunisia,' I said. 'She always wanted to go there for some reason.'

Trick looked impressed, so I told him more, about how she was living in the van and camping, stopping at places with names like Qalibiyah and Qurbus.

I looked at our hands stroking the dead crop.

'D'you think it's weird?'

'Not for country people,' he said, and seeing my blank face, he explained. 'You know, you lot. The settled community, brick-lovers. Stationary folk. Country people always leave each other . . .

'Sorry,' he added, and I wondered if I'd flinched.

'And you lot don't?'

He shook his head. 'Think some of them wish they would,' he said. He dug his nail into the ground leaving a little crescent there.

'Know what we call you?' he said.

'What?'

'*Gorgios.*'

He looked at me, delighted.

'Am I supposed to be offended?'

He shrugged as if that were up to me, then started telling me about the *gorgios* that lived behind him for a bit when he was growing up. They all had the same clothes, he said.

'White trainers and tracky bottoms. And they were shit-scared of us!'

I wrinkled my nose. 'Doubt it.'

He started talking about how things used to be different, and how travellers used to be welcome. When he was older he wanted to live in the old way, he said: cooking over a fire and living off the land and sleeping under the stars. He talked more about travelling the world, and the places he would go, and I listened happily, imagining myself out there too, driving around in a sky blue van.

'So, why'd she go, then? Your mammy?'

I looked at him, surprised, but his face was so friendly and open. I breathed in slowly, and thought about it.

'She used to get really angry,' I said, after a while. 'She said she didn't want us growing up with her like that. That we're better off . . . She said she didn't want to blame us.'

'*Blame* you?' he said, and I shrugged.

He asked why I hadn't gone with her.

'*I* would have,' he said, and I thought of Sam and how much he'd wanted to go.

I said it was because of school, because that seemed easiest, but really I wouldn't have gone because of Dad. I didn't tell him that she hadn't wanted us.

'Our ma gets pretty angry,' he said. 'But we just ignore her.'

'There was no way you could ignore mine.'

'My da's like that,' he said. 'Happiest man in the world most of the time, but when he goes . . .'

He looked like he was going to say something else, so I stayed quiet and waited, but he only plucked a dandelion, leaves and all, and rolled it into a scrappy ball.

Lying next to him like that, I thought of an old picture of Mum and Dad. They are leaning on each other, laughing, in front of a caravan. He's in flares and she's

34

in a flowery minidress. She only looks a few years older than me. They were a boy and a girl, like us right now. I didn't understand. How was it possible to *stop* loving someone?

I stood up, brushing the dirt off my shorts, and asked Trick if he wanted to see something cool, which, of course, he did.

If you followed the brook deep into the Ashbourne Estate, right to the furthest edge of the cornfield, past where the Shetland ponies feed in the meadow and the barbed wire is snagged with sheep's wool, you eventually came to Drum Hill, which the brook flowed through inside a concrete tunnel.

I let Trick go in front so he could see the view from the top first.

He whistled in appreciation.

Ashbourne Lake spread out below us, big as a football pitch and glittering in the sun. A pair of swans came in to land as we reached the water's edge, scattering moorhens with their floppy orange feet. Trick kicked water at them, making them hiss, and I told him to leave them alone. I laughed a minute later when one waddled onto the bank and went snapping and hissing after him.

The right-hand verge was striped with an orchard, and I collapsed under a gnarled-looking apple tree, desperate for shade. In the background, Ashbourne Hall stood grey and square, and Trick asked if we were allowed to be here. I told him that we'd have to run if anyone came, and he didn't say anything, but I could see from his profile that he was pleased.

At the lake's centre, a stone woman poured water over her bare shoulders, and I found myself falling into thinking about Mum again, the way she used to wet a sponge in the bath and squeeze it so water ran over her head, wetting her long hair. Before I fell any further, I kicked off my shoes and ran into the freezing water.

Everything was muffled and reeds tickled my belly, and then there was a fizzing noise and Trick had jumped in beside me. We trod water, and grinned at each other because it was impossible to describe how good it was to have sun hot on our scalps, and water cold on our bodies, and the surface flashing gold and silver every time we turned our heads.

A bolt of electric blue caught my eye, and I tracked it automatically, moving slowly through the water.

'What is it?' Trick asked, following behind me.

'*Shhh.*'

The damselfly flitted from reed to reed then stopped. Its wings moved so fast they almost disappeared.

'It *is*! Look. I can't believe it! It's an azure damselfly! I thought I'd never see one.'

The rod-like body twitched, then took off, and I flung water into the air to celebrate.

'How can you tell?' Trick asked, and he looked

confused by how excited I was, but he wasn't trying to make me feel stupid, so I told him the truth: because of my dad.

'The azure's got three stripes on its thorax. They're really rare. My dad knows everything about plants and animals,' I said, flicking water at a mist of gnats.

'Cool,' Trick said, and I ducked my head under the water so I could beam unwitnessed.

Emerging straight-faced, I hooked my toes against a stone on the bank. Trick did the same.

'I'm glad we came here,' he announced, and I knew from his voice that he didn't just mean today and to the lake.

'Me too,' I told him, and my hair swirled around my ears in agreement.

Four

We hung around together every day after that. It was so hot there was a hosepipe ban, and I snuck a wonky stool out from Silverweed, which we used to play cards in the shade under the oak tree. Trick was an Irish traveller, which meant he was Catholic, and supposed to go to Mass a lot more than he did, and, of course, that he was Irish, though he'd only been to Dublin once since he was born there and couldn't remember it.

Sometimes people who love talking are no good at listening, but it wasn't that way with Trick. He paid attention, and I told him everything. I talked a lot about Mum. He was the only person I knew who was impressed by what she was doing. I told him how she loved singing, and how easily she laughed, and how easily she shouted, and what she looked like when she got all done up for a night out with Tess – how she would wear all black and

38

no make-up except lipstick, and her hair would be piled on top of her head.

He showed me how to dig under fire embers to bake corn on the cob, and told me about past evictions. If it was a big one, with lots of families, everyone did their bit, even the little ones. They'd pull at the men's legs, and cry. They'd end up getting pushed over or shoved aside, which would send the mums mad, though they should just have kept them safely indoors in the first place.

If Trick's dad knew the bailiffs were coming, he'd get his brothers in. There were six of them. In the past, there had been proper stand-offs, bricks thrown and windows smashed and fires set. Trick's eyes lit up when he told me the extent they'd go to to stand their ground against the *gorgios*. It made me feel weird, listening to the stories.

He told me that his Uncle Johnny, the one with the enormous chin, had his trailer burned down once, and I couldn't believe it. Someone actually set it on fire? For no reason? Trick said country people did stuff like that all the time.

'They don't like us when we travel, they don't like us when we stop,' he said.

Dad was still waiting for the council to agree to help him with an eviction. Once they agreed, the travellers basically had to remove themselves, or face The

Consequences, which as far as I could tell meant being moved by force or, if they resisted, being moved by force *and* being arrested and having their vehicles and trailers confiscated.

I thought it sounded cruel, but Dad said I didn't understand. 'You think everybody's good,' he said, like I was some kind of idiot because I didn't want to make people live on the dual carriageway. 'You watch. They'll stay here for as long as they can, make a bleeding mess, and clear off. And who d'you think's going to sort out their rubbish?'

Me and Trick didn't talk about the feud. As far as I could tell, neither of us had any say in the matter, so there wasn't much point. Instead, we swam in the lake, climbed the oak tree, built fires, ate corn, and talked about everything else, and just as it was getting to the point that I couldn't remember what life had been like without him, a phone call to Silverweed came and reminded me.

'Have I done something to upset you?' Matty burst out on the 'o' of my 'Hello'.

I'd almost forgotten she existed.

'I thought you'd ring, or ask me round or *something*. Have we fallen out?'

'Course we haven't,' I said. 'It's only been a week.'

'Two!' she said. '*Nearly*. Last year we spent the whole holiday together *and* we spoke on the phone every day.'

I felt bad. Matty was right. Last year we had spent all summer together. And every summer for four years before that. Benjy and Matty would come over loads and we'd sit in the garden drawing, or take sandwiches out to the paddock. Sometimes Matty would watch from her towel as we rode an inflated inner tube down the brook.

I apologised, and she exhaled, sending vibrations down the phone.

'Why don't you come round, then? On Saturday.'

'No,' she said. 'You come here. Tomorrow. They do the shopping on Fridays.'

'Great,' I said, but I had a feeling of dread.

I ran a bath for Fiasco, because she'd been rolling in fox shit again, and because it always made me laugh to see her desperate expression when I rubbed soap on her long brown ears. She jumped out midway and soaked the bathroom, and I could hardly lift her back in – she was so heavy when wet. I was in the middle of cleaning up the mess she'd made when there was a knock at the front door.

Nobody used the front. I shouted for whoever it was to come round the back, and I was so surprised to see Punky Beresford standing there that I didn't even say hello. A tall, skinny girl in a baseball cap was with him. I hadn't seen her before. She held a growling pit bull by its collar. Fiasco barked her head off, still damp

41

from her bath, but she didn't come out from behind my legs.

'Is Sam in?' Punky said.

I shook my head. I didn't even know they knew each other. Punky Beresford had been in the year above Sam. He was expelled last year before he took his exams for throwing a chair through a window in the maths block.

He had the bluest eyes in the world. They were pink at the edges, like he'd just been crying – though you couldn't imagine it – and he stared at you when he talked, so it felt like a challenge. His front teeth overlapped slightly, and the left tooth had a grey patch in the middle where the nerve had died, but it didn't make him ugly. Even the story that went with it, that his dad had hit him in the face with a television, couldn't do that.

The girl had high cheekbones dented with acne scars, and black hair cut into a bob. One side curled under her chin and the other hung straight down, so it looked uneven. I had to shout over the racket the dogs were making. I told them Sam wasn't in, that he was off somewhere with Benjy, though I had no idea really, and when I was finished, Punky gave me this strange, slow smile. He tilted his head back when he spoke, and those pink and blue eyes stared.

He said to tell Sam he'd be at the rec later, and he spoke even slower than he smiled, so I couldn't tell if he was stoned, or taking the piss out of me somehow.

'I like your dog,' the girl said, and her voice was really soft and high-pitched, like a little kid's. She let go of the pit bull's collar, and her and Punky walked off, holding hands. From the kitchen I could hear the dog's claws tapping on the path.

Five

Matty answered the door in black hot pants and a silver bikini.

'I've been in the garden since seven,' she gasped, giving Dad and Austin a little wave as they drove off in the pick-up. Dad gave her a nod, but Austin only looked away.

Ever since Dad took him on last year, Austin had been in love with Matty. He was so shy around her that she called him The Mute. She wouldn't believe me when I told her how clever he was about trees and ponds and plants. She said he was just like a Labrador with his scraggy hair and sad eyes. Nice to pat occasionally but you wouldn't have him in the house.

'It's sweltering!' she said now.

I'd never heard her say sweltering before.

'What've you got on?' she said, looking at my baggy jeans and T-shirt. 'You'll die like that.'

'Nah,' I said, my legs already sweating inside the thick denim. Death was better than comments about why it wasn't normal to wear my mum's dirty running shorts, and why I should be sympathetic if Dad couldn't face doing the laundry.

'Donna's got loads of stuff in,' Matty said, and I didn't ask why she'd started using her mum's first name.

The kitchen gleamed white. If you made toast at Matty's house, you had to get the toaster out of a cupboard, and then – before you'd even taken a bite – you had to return it, and wipe the crumbs from the surface. If you really wanted to make Donna mad, you just had to leave the toaster out, or eat *without using a plate*.

The back door was open, and a bright line of sequin- and diamanté-studded flip-flops waited beside it: glamorous boats at the pontoon. Matty dropped ice and slices of lime into a jug, filled it with ginger beer, and I listened to the fizz rising. She got three glasses and put everything onto a tray.

'Carry that out for me?' she said, stepping into her flip-flops, and before I thought to ask why *she* didn't take it, I was following her with the loaded tray into the garden.

Donna was sunbathing. 'I-*ris*!' she called. 'Perfect timing with the fizz!'

I set it down on the white patio table.

'Come here, *you*,' she said, like I was her long-lost daughter. Her body smelled of orchids and was smothered in oil, and I tried not to feel uncomfortable in the heat radiating from it as I leaned down to kiss her cheek.

'What *have* you got on?' she said. 'Matty, go and find Iris something decent – she'll swelter like that.'

'Oh, I'm fine,' I said. 'I only burn anyway.'

'No. Off you go. I can't bear looking at you!'

I thought of Trick waiting in the field, and how it would only take ten minutes to get there if I ran, but I followed Matty up to her bedroom. It was like a wasp spilling pheromones to an ant; as soon as I was anywhere near her I lost all initiative.

'Sorry,' Matty said, as she rifled through drawer after drawer. 'She just worries about you.'

'I'm fine.'

Matty passed me a pair of sunset-covered Bermuda shorts. They slouched on my hips, ending below my knees.

'My uncle brought them back from Florida,' she told me. 'They look good.'

I raised my eyebrows at her. 'I look like a beach towel.'

She laughed. 'Everything else still has the tags in.'

In the last few months Matty had shot up six inches – an average willy size, as Donna liked to say – so Donna had bought her a whole new wardrobe.

'Take those home with you,' Matty said.

'What? *You* don't want them?'

Back in the garden, Donna lay on her sunbed doing a crossword. She put her pen down, and frowned at my shorts.

'You are a measly host, Mats,' she said, laughing. 'At least let Iris have your lounger.'

Matty shifted to the grass between us. The floral padding was damp from her sweat.

'So . . .' Donna prompted, her brown eyes full of mischief.

Up close, her liquid eyeliner was wonky. Black crumbs were scattered in the creases under her eyes. I lay back, remembering what Mum had said about not having to answer people's questions.

Noises came from the gardens that surrounded us: a lawnmower, a metal bin lid crashing shut, cutlery scraping a plate. A bunch of kids somewhere shrieked.

Trick would be in the cornfields now, or swimming in the lake. He'd have given up waiting for me. I imagined introducing him to Matty, bumping into her as the two of us wandered through the village, chatting away like we had since we first met. Trick would be friendly but detached, perking up whenever he spoke to me . . .

Matty prodded one of my sunsets. '*Iris*. Donna's talking to you.'

47

'I said, how are *things*?' Donna repeated. 'Dad all right?'

'Yeah, he's fine, thanks.'

'Still drinking at The Stag?'

'Yep.'

'And he's all right, is he?'

'Yeah, fine. Thanks.'

'And he's got enough work on?'

'Yeah, he's got a big job on at the minute. A load of dying elms, somewhere out by the Peaks.'

'Oh wonderful!' she said. 'One less thing to worry about. And how about your bro?'

She watched me over her glass as she sipped.

'I love his hair long,' Matty gushed. 'D'you think he'll keep growing it?'

I took a swig of ginger beer and shrugged.

'Saw him a few nights ago. With that awful big lad, he was,' Donna said. 'That one whose mum's in the madhouse. You know. The one with the daft name.'

She squinted, trying to remember, and I thought *Punky, Punky, Punky*. She gave up.

'Sam's not in with him, is he?' Donna said.

I shook my head so they'd both stop examining me.

'Bad lad, that one. Does your dad know?'

I nodded automatically. I hated the way Donna acted like my dad was the only parent in the world who didn't know everything his kids got up to. As soon as Matty got a boyfriend she planned to have sex with him so she could be the first girl in our form to do it. Did Donna know about that?

She got up and refilled our glasses, and she obviously couldn't read minds because she said, 'Mats's got a new boyfriend, haven't you, doll?'

Matty sat up, enthusiastic suddenly. 'Oh Iris! It's that boy from the pet shop. I told him I loved fish!'

I pulled a face at her.

'I know! I panicked. You've *got* to help me. I said I loved the little freaks. He works in the aquarium section. *He's sixteen!*' She whispered the last two words in case they blew my mind.

We lay there like this until all the ginger beer had vanished, and when Donna brought out tuna sandwiches I felt a familiar pang because she'd cut the crusts off, and shaken crisps onto each plate, and I had to tense my stomach for a few seconds to make the ache go away. I focused on Trick jumping into Ashbourne Lake, and his tanned body drying off on the bank beside me, and the cornfield stretching out blondly for miles all around.

When the plates were washed and dried and put away, and the sides wiped down and the tea towels hung on the rail to dry, me and Matty went upstairs. She experimented with bright blue eye make-up and went on about how fit the pet-shop boy was, and all the things he had done that made her think he really liked her, and I lay on her bed, staring at the leftover Blu-Tack on the ceiling. I remembered the day we'd stuck neon plastic stars there, last December. Matty had bossed me about, rearranging each one I touched.

'The thing about you, Iris, is that you haven't got any flair,' she'd told me, and I'd gone to sit by her window, looking out at the snow, wondering where I could get some.

I thought of Trick's expression when I'd shown him the azure damselfly, and I wondered what he was doing precisely this second. He would know I wasn't coming by now.

'Iris!' Matty said. 'You're rubbish today . . .'

She swung around to face me, almost singing as she repeated whatever it was I was supposed to be listening to.

'*What* should I *say* if he *asks* what I *feed my fish*?'

I sat up. Her mouth was open as she waited for me to answer.

'Why did you invite me round today, Matty?'

'Huh?'

'Why did you invite me round?' Propped on the edge of her bed, I forced myself not to look away. One of her brown eyes was ringed with a sparkling blue, and it made her look vulnerable somehow, like a panda dressed up for a disco.

She shook her head, laughing at me. '*Iris . . .*'

'I just wonder.'

Her amusement was turning to hurt. 'We're friends, aren't we?'

The sun through the window made her silky black hair shine, and she gathered it up in her hands, brought it to rest on the opposite shoulder.

'We've been best friends forever . . .' she said, sounding less certain.

'Then why did you give me these horrible shorts?'

'Because you were hot!' she said.

'And why do you always tell me what you think of my clothes? And my personality. My *family*, even. Why d'you think you can do that?'

She stood up. '*God*. What's wrong with you today? You've been rude all morning . . .'

'*I've* been rude!' I gasped, and I was about to launch into a rant, but I stopped myself. I didn't want to argue. I just wanted things to change.

'Suppose it doesn't feel much like *best friends* to me any more.'

Matty came to sit beside me on the bed. Her eyes were soft now, and I wondered if I'd made a mistake, because she could be so nice, and gentle, but then she said, in her softest talk-show voice, 'Is this because of your mum?' and she looked so sympathetic I wanted to punch her in the face.

51

'It's nothing to do with my stupid mum, Matty. *God!* That isn't the only thing that's ever happened to me, you know.'

She widened her eyes. 'Soz, Iris, no need to go mental.'

'Maybe *I've* got a boyfriend,' I said. 'Can you even imagine that?'

'What?' she said, and then her eyes narrowed to slits. 'Who, that gypsy? *Iris.*'

'You don't know anything about it,' I said.

I started pulling my jeans back on. 'And you can have your weird shorts back and all.'

'Where're you going?' she called after me, but I didn't answer because I was taking the stairs two at a time, then I was out the front door, tearing down her road, adrenalin rushing through me.

I leaped up and grabbed a handful of sycamore leaves, disturbing a pigeon by mistake. Its grey wings beat the air as it flew into the cloudless sky, and I felt something inside me taking off with it.

Six

The next morning, I went out early. By the time I'd got to the corn den after Matty's yesterday, Trick had gone and I wanted to see him. I couldn't resist stopping at my trusty alder to spy on his family. Across the ditch, his dad stared into the fire, finishing off a cup of something.

The sky was still pale, and his squat shadow fell onto the caravan behind him. There was a bandage on the knuckle of his right hand, and his thick neck and shoulders were sunburned, and I would never admit it, but he scared me. What would he say if he saw me, watching him like this? I didn't dare move.

I could hear the brook, and I willed Trick's dad to turn his back for ten seconds so I could run. I wanted to be there and safe, in the mud and wild garlic of the bank, and the moss of the stepping stones, feeling the cool air by the water. He tipped his cup out onto the grass and walked into the caravan, and I made a run for it.

Sunlight stabbed through ash and willow to make a spotlight on the stepping stones, and I basked there for a moment, catching my breath and warming my face. Two chub slid beneath the surface of the brownish water. Minnows scattered. An emperor dragonfly bobbed above the surface.

I ran through the corridor to the corn den. Thick green stalks brushed my shoulders, and I crossed my fingers, nervous in case Trick was or wasn't there.

'Iris,' he said, lifting himself on his elbows.

'Eh up,' I said, and relief tingled the back of my neck. I dropped down cross-legged, and pulled a sweating bottle of pop from my rucksack. I'd bought it on my way home from Matty's with the money Dad had given me for chips. It had been in the fridge all night. The bottle gasped open, and I took a big drink then passed it over.

All around us the corn made a grinding, shifting sound, and I settled on my side, temple on palm, thinking of all the insects drinking and feeding around us.

'Where were you yesterday?' he asked, and I apologised.

'Had to go to my stupid friend's house. I came here after, but you'd gone.'

He passed the pop back.

'Ever had a friend who made you feel like a dickhead all the time?'

Trick lay back without answering.

'You in a mood with me?' I said, and started explaining how I hadn't wanted to go to Matty's in the first place, but he shook his head.

I stared beyond our feet to the corridor, and the bamboo-like maize stems, and the different shades of green, but still he didn't say anything, and so I asked if he went to the lake, like we'd planned.

'Nah,' he said. 'Couldn't be arsed.'

He relaxed into his usual position – flip-flops off, hands behind his head – but he seemed different, and after a while I realised why: his feet were tapping the air constantly, as if he had itchy bones. Usually, he lay lizard-still.

I asked him if he was all right, and he nodded, but I knew he wasn't telling the truth.

'It's me da . . .' he said, finally. He sat up, wrapped his arms round his knees, and focused on a bunch of ragwort near his toes. 'He found out that I haven't . . .'

He pulled at his top lip, and the field was so quiet I heard the kissing sound it made as it suckered his gums.

'What?'

He glanced at me, then back at the ragwort. 'He found out I haven't been going to school.'

I was confused. Of course he hadn't been going to school, it was the summer holidays.

'I mean, he found out I've been *chucked out* of school.'

'Oh. But you said—'

'I know,' he said, meeting my eyes properly for the first time. 'Let me tell you what happened.'

I plucked an ear of corn because my heart was thudding against my chest and I needed something to fiddle with so I could listen properly.

'Me da wasn't bothered about me going in the first place, he wanted me to go to work with him – thinks school's a waste of time after a bit.'

The corn felt cool and unfamiliar as I passed it between my sticky hands. Trick seemed nervous and defensive – completely unlike he'd been before – and I couldn't work out if it was because of what he had to tell me or because he was lying.

'It was okay for a bit,' he said. 'For ages, actually. Just normal. People left me alone, or were friendly; I liked it. I played footy at break, it was all right. Then this lad, my year, got attacked by someone. *Gypsy*, he said, and the way he acted, you'd think it was me who did it. Matt *Dunbar*. A big, blond, sporty bastard. Him and his mates started shouting at me at break, trying to get me to fight.'

I saw Year Tens doing this kind of thing to younger boys all the time, but it was hard to imagine Trick as the victim.

'In the end, I got angry because he kept saying it was . . .' He stopped talking, but his feet kept tapping, left then right, and I wanted to put my hands on them, to make them stop because they were distracting me.

'Go on,' I said.

I dismantled the corn on the cob, making a food pile for the pheasants.

'Well, Matt Dunbar's giving it *backwards pikey scumbag* and all that, and none of the teachers notice, or give a toss, and I'm not too bothered neither, till he starts calling me a pussy. Says *pikeys* only fight when they know they can win, as if I wouldn't dare fight him! And every time I refuse, it gets worse. So one day I just have enough, and when he asks me for a fight, I punch him straight in the eyes.'

'Well, yeah,' I said. 'So what?' I knew people like Matt Dunbar, and the only thing that made them stop was a smack in the eyes.

'But I shouldn't have, Iris, that's the thing, because I *know* how to fight. I'm not being big-headed or nothing, but I was bred for it. Me da taught me, and I kind of hate it but . . .'

'*Bred* for it?'

I felt as though a curtain had been pulled back to reveal a whole world I didn't know about, right here in England, in this little town. In my back garden.

'He used to be a bare-knuckle fighter, for years – you should see his hands, they're a holy mess, fat bendy sausage fingers . . .' He pulled a face, as if the sausages

57

were coming for him. 'Hates them now he's stopped, they won't do what he wants, but he used to be over the moon. They were his pride and joy when I was growing up.'

'Is it legal?'

'Nah, but no one cares. Rozzers leave us to it. Me da was one of the big boys, no one beat Paddy Delaney. I wanted to be just like him. I started to have my own reputation at the old camp. But I got fed up of it too. It never ends! I don't see the point. I don't want to fight any more, but it's like I don't have a choice. I tell my ma, it comes for me, I swear! But I should never have fought a *gorgia*. Not the way I did. No offence.'

'So what happened?'

He looked at me, pulling at his top lip. 'He was a big lad, you know, Iris, hardest in Year Ten . . .'

'*Trick*.'

'I punched him and he went down, and his face smacked on the tarmac – school tarmac, no less – and knocked his front teeth out. I gave him a bit of a kicking, you know, then I ran off.'

He didn't sound proud or sorry as he spoke, just matter of fact. I wondered how I would do in a fight.

'I hear later he had to staý overnight in the hospital. Concussion and all that. He's all right now, though,' he added quickly.

'So how d'you know you're expelled?'

He looked puzzled.

'They can't expel you without asking for your side. *At least.* Kids at my school stay on for worse than that.'

'Trust me, Iris. I wrecked it. And now me da says it's work with him. Don't come crying to me, he said . . .'

'And you did?'

'Course I friggin' didn't, but he found out anyway – he finds out everything – and now he's spitting because he told me what'd happen, told me not to get mixed up with . . .' He stopped, but it was obvious what he'd been about to say.

'I just thought if I waited till the new term, everything'd calm down, and they might let me back in, and I wouldn't have to tell him, or you, or go to work. It doesn't really matter cause I'm gonna work for myself, but I don't know. I liked it at school.'

He ran out of words, and he looked so dejected that I couldn't help reaching out to him. I stroked his knee, as if he were a pet that had just come back from an operation.

'Matt Dunbar sounds like a prick,' I told him. 'I'm glad you beat him up. You should have told me though. I tell *you* everything.'

'I know,' he said, and he smiled at me, full whack. 'That's why I like you, Iris. I can talk to you about anything.'

I shrugged because I couldn't trust myself to speak.

'And you're pretty,' he added, really quickly, and I almost laughed out loud with the joy of it.

I wished there were some way Matty could have witnessed this.

When the energy shooting around my bloodstream had calmed down, I asked what he was going to do.

'What can I do? Hole up here for a bit, then go face him.'

Babyish ideas entered my head, like *You could hide in the chicken coop*, or *Camp in the cornfields*, or *We could run away together*, but I managed to keep them inside.

Trick said he was on driving duties, for lying, which meant he wouldn't be able to get out for a while, and I tried not to look shocked that his dad would let him drive a car about before he was even fifteen. We arranged to meet in a few days' time, on Wednesday, at nine p.m. If he wasn't there by ten, it meant he couldn't get out.

'I'll just come back the next night,' I said.

And the night after that.

And the night after that.

Trick couldn't relax, but he didn't want to go home, and so we headed to the brook to cool our feet.

At the ancient oak, I heard something.

'Wait,' I said, raising a finger.

We cocked our heads.

'There,' I said, and he nodded.

'You're not wrong.'

It was Dad. And he was shouting my name.

Seven

Clearing the pig farmer's gate, I heard Dad shout again. I kicked up dust as I ran down the lane. Through the wispy branches of the poplars surrounding our yard, I could see him, fingers at his mouth, about to whistle. I shouted, and he stalked to meet me on the drive.

'Where the *bleeding* hell have you been?'

'Nowhere.'

'Nowhere? I've been shouting all morning.'

My pulse throbbed at my temple.

'Austin's out looking for you.'

'Why?' I asked in a small voice, thinking of Sam and Mum and rubber skid marks across busy roads.

'Some stuff from the shed's gone missing,' he said, heading for the house. 'I need you to wait in, in case the coppers call back.'

'Wait in?' I followed behind him. 'Where are you going?'

'Blasted chainsaw's banjaxed again. Austin's driving me into town. Haven't got time to waste, waiting around for the bloody phone to ring.'

'Have you spoken to Sam? Maybe he borrowed something?'

'Course I flaming have,' he said. 'Though God knows what he'd want with a monkey wrench, he can't even wash his bleeding football kit. Anyway, the window's smashed at the back.'

I shut up. I didn't know what there was to say anyway, I just wanted to slow things down.

'I told you this would happen, didn't I?' he went on, in the kitchen now. 'I said so. They wouldn't bloody listen.'

'Who?'

'Who d'you think? Bloody coppers! What did they expect?'

I sat at the kitchen table while he hunted around the kitchen for the pick-up keys. They hung off a bundle of keyrings Sam and me had brought him back from different school trips, but he still managed to lose them every day.

'*Iris!*' he shouted, out of nowhere. 'That *bloody* foot . . .'

I stood up and stared at him. My eyes prickled as if there were little stags behind them, charging. I wasn't upset, I was angry, and I wanted him to notice me for once, but he was focused on the phone, like that would solve all his problems.

I stamped upstairs, dragging my finger through the dust on the banister. He hadn't even tried to keep things nice. I sank into the armchair in his room, not caring that he was in and might catch me. I wanted to see what Trick's mum and his little sisters were doing in the paddock.

I didn't expect to see Trick. He must have decided to come out from the cornfield straight away, because he was slumped by the fire with his mum and little sisters, eating something. They looked just like a family on a camping holiday.

I was angry because stuff got nicked all the time. Just because it hadn't happened to us before didn't mean it was never going to. It could've been anyone. But Dad would make out I was stupid if I even suggested something like that. He thought I was so gullible.

Trick's mum was handing some drinks out. She moved like Trick, swift and precise. He was nothing like his dad at all. The way he hunched over to lace his boots, ignoring everybody, his thick neck sloping to meet his shoulders. My stomach dropped when I thought of him. Trick smiled at something his mum said and I just knew it, I felt it. *He wouldn't steal from us.*

Beyond the travellers, on the Ashbourne Estate, the maize flowers rippled prettily. I pictured the corn den, empty, and wished we were back there, just the two of us, without all this.

Trick's mum chucked him an apple and he bit into it, looking tense as he waited for his dad to get home. I wanted to warn him about what was happening. I wanted him to be prepared.

'Eye?'

Dad's voice made me jump, and I pretended to be rooting through the washing pile on the armchair. He held out a cup of tea, and I took it without saying thanks.

'Look at all that rubbish,' he tutted, coming to stand beside me.

Black sacks and some tied-up carrier bags were piled at the back of each caravan, and one of the dogs, or a fox, had ripped out the insides. Food cartons and nappies were strewn about the paddock. There were piles of old tyres and sheets of corrugated iron and an empty gas canister by the fire.

'You didn't answer me before,' he said.

Neither of us looked at the other, and I listened for clues in his voice about whether or not I was in trouble.

'Where were you? When I shouted.'

I blew on my tea, making the surface move: Ashbourne Lake in the breeze.

'Iris?'

'Pig farmer's field,' I lied.

65

'Then why didn't you hear me?'

'Must've fallen asleep.'

He looked worried, which meant he'd decided to talk to me about something, and I crossed my fingers so hard my knuckle joints hurt that it wasn't anything that would stop me from seeing Trick.

He shifted his weight from left to right hip then tidied up the towers of five pences he was collecting on the windowsill.

'Look. I know I've been letting you run wild lately, but it's only because I trust you. I don't worry about you like I do your brother. I know you're sensible.'

I picked a cat hair from my tea.

'Leave that alone a sec, I want to talk to you. About the gypsies . . .'

Irish travellers, I corrected secretly.

I braced myself for him to say he knew about my friendship with Trick, and that I wasn't allowed out by myself any more because I couldn't be trusted, because I was as bad as my blasted brother, and worse than my mum, but he only said, 'I know what you're like, Eye, you see the best in people, and it's a lovely thing, but . . .' He turned away from me, nodded towards the paddock. 'I've been in the world a long time, and those people down there, you can't trust them. And I know you think I'm being unfair, or *prejudiced*,' he said, as though prejudiced wasn't a real word, 'and I know you feel sorry for them – I've *seen* you watching – but they're not like us. They're parasites, Eye. It's what they do.'

I uncrossed my fingers then because it was obvious that he didn't know a thing, and I realised that even if I did tell him the truth – that Trick was my friend, and that he'd never steal from us, that I *knew* him – he wouldn't take my word for it. He *couldn't*.

'I was wrong to let it stand for so long,' he said. 'They bite the hand that feeds them, I think everyone agrees about that. Come here.'

He opened his arms out for a cuddle, and I stepped inside, inhaling his warm smell of wool and sweat and grass.

'Don't like you thinking I'm a pig, Eye,' he said, and his voice was gruff again like it always was when he admitted something, and I told him that I didn't think he was a pig, which surprised both of us, because he *was* prejudiced, *and* he thought I was too silly to decide anything for myself, but I meant it.

Eight

The police stuck to their word. By nine-thirty a.m. on Monday two officers – WPC Baker and PC Todd – were standing in the kitchen looking as though they couldn't quite believe they'd come all the way down this potholed lane for not much missing from a tree surgeon's shed.

It turned out that as well as the window at the back being smashed, and Dad's monkey wrench having gone, a claw hammer was missing, and a stretch of thick chain. I wondered if Trick had heard anything, but I saw him on Saturday. He would have said.

Dad gave the police cups of his finest cabbage water. He loved giving officials weak tea; he put a single tea bag in the pot, and filled it right to the top so that when you added milk it turned grey. Once he did it to Nanny Ferris, and Mum noticed and went mental.

PC Todd read Dad's statement back to him, and when he reached the bit where Dad finds the tools missing, he looked up, as if to check Dad's reaction. Dad looked straight back, the heel of his work boot resting against the Aga. Between me and Dad, Fiasco's tail twitched.

PC Todd was getting to the end of the statement when the door opened and Sam walked in. I stared at his head. All his brown curls had gone. I could smell his shower gel and deodorant as he walked past, and I watched for Dad's reaction to his shaved head. PC Todd nodded an acknowledgement, but Sam just took a seat on the bench by the phone, straightening out his Adidas Stripes. His face was blotchy from having the shower on too hot.

WPC Baker was furthest away. She hadn't said anything since she'd introduced herself and plonked her bum on the edge of the table. Now she watched Sam. He looked bored. He was rubbing his little finger across the full moon scar he had on his forehead. It had been there since he was a toddler: a decapitated chicken pock. He used to fiddle with it at the same time as he sucked his thumb, until Mum started covering his nail in this ointment that tasted like earwax.

PC Todd took a pen from behind his ear, and clicked it open against his clipboard.

'And you're certain that when you locked the shed nothing was missing?'

'Nothing missing. Nothing smashed,' Dad said.

PC Todd's trousers were a half-shiny navy blue, like Sam's school trousers. It didn't seem right they should be so similar.

'And how about the children? Were you two around that night? You didn't hear anything, see anything?' he said.

Dad looked at us. He'd been at the Stag. Friday was always a late one.

I shook my head. 'I was in, but I didn't notice anything.'

'I was at my friend's house,' Sam said.

Todd wrote our answers down.

'It's like I said on the phone. There're gypsies down the paddock. A whole load of them. A lad, two men—'

'We're not here to talk about the eviction, Mr Dancy,' Baker interrupted. 'Far as we're concerned, this is an entirely separate case.'

Dad made a scoffing sound. 'We'll see about that,' he said. He threw an amused look at Fiasco, who seemed to grin back.

WPC Baker looked annoyed.

'Will you need statements off them?' Dad asked, meaning me and Sam.

I held WPC Baker's gaze, though my throat was tight at the thought of her watching me with those grave blue eyes.

'That depends on whether either of them have any information,' Baker said, and her voice was devoid of expression as she looked at each of us. I stroked Fiasco and tried to look sweet.

Silence filled the room, and I got that feeling, like when you're watching a play and you're not sure who's meant to speak next, that the pause was for dramatic effect, or because someone had forgotten their lines.

I nudged Fiasco with my foot to set her tail wagging again. Sam stroked his little moon absently. His head gleamed. He looked like a different person. I hated it.

'Could we have a word, Mr Dancy?' Baker said finally.

Without being told, me and Sam left the kitchen. I walked to my bedroom then crept back to listen at the kitchen door, expecting Sam to do the same, but his heavy footsteps up to his room hadn't been for show.

'There's been a period of over . . .' Todd paused. Paper flicked. 'Three weeks, with the gypsies present, and no criminal activity—'

'Except for the illegal squatting,' Dad interrupted. 'And the fly-tipping. And God knows how much of my wood they're chucking on the fire.'

Baker intervened, 'As I said earlier, we aren't here to discuss your plans to evict today, Mr Dancy.'

She had a weird way of talking, emphasising the wrong words, as if she'd got bored of saying the same things all the time. 'We're here to talk about the break-in to your shed.'

'I think you'll find the two are quite closely related,' Dad said.

'We'll be the judge of that.'

'And you say this is the first time anything like this has happened down here?' Todd said.

'In *fifteen years*,' Dad said, and there was another silence, a longer one this time, until Baker spoke again.

'You know, the last time we ran into you, Mr Dancy, you were hiding, half-cut, in the back of your car. We had to take you in to do a little blood test. Are you *managing* to get to work okay?'

She was talking about when Dad got done for drunk driving. It wasn't long after Mum left, and I didn't know what had happened, just that Dad wasn't allowed to drive any more. That was why Austin had gone from part-time helper to full-time apprentice, so he could drive the pick-up as well.

The kitchen tap dripped, and I wondered what Dad's face was doing.

'The fact is, without any evidence, this break-in may not strengthen your case with the council at all,' Baker said.

'Couldn't bloody weaken it.'

'I wouldn't be so sure, Mr Dancy. This *could* be construed as sabotage.'

Dad made a strangled noise.

'All we're saying is, there're proper channels for dealing with these situations,' Todd put in.

'Oh don't get me started on your flaming channels,' Dad said. He stopped himself, and when he spoke again his voice had changed completely.

'Righty-ho then. I know where I stand.' The back door creaked open.

'Wish we could be of more help, Mr Dancy, but the fact is—' Baker sing-songed.

'Don't worry, love. Got it. Loud and clear.'

There was some shuffling as the police left, and Fiasco jumped onto the table to bark at them as they walked to the shed.

That afternoon, I found Dad sitting in the living room, watching telly with the sound off. He never watched telly in the daytime, except for at Christmas.

The living room curtains were closed, but there was a gap in the middle where they didn't quite meet. Mum had talked about replacing them ever since she shrank them in the wash last year. I promised that as soon as I had some money, I would do it myself.

Sunlight pierced through the gap, turning bits of dust to glitter. Fiasco lay on Dad's feet with her head on her paws. I sat in the chair next to them. Her tail thumped the floor in greeting.

'You all right, Dad?'

'Not really, Eye. I'm fed up.'

I scrunched my mouth over to one side, trying to think of something to say.

The walls in the living room were exactly like rice pudding except for being a pale green. I reached out to touch them, feeling the familiar lumps. Stuck to the ceiling above Dad's seat was a dollop of tomato sauce of which all three of us had denied knowledge. I looked up at it.

'I'll clean that tomorrow,' I said.

Dad blew air out his nose.

The remote control had fallen from the arm of Dad's chair, and lay on the floor with its batteries nearby. I leaned down and picked them up.

'What you watching?' I said.

'Sharks.'

'Cool,' I said.

I looped the elastic band that secured the back around the remote and handed it to him. He tapped his finger on the buttons.

'That was the pig who took my licence,' he said, and I did my best That's News To Me face. 'Sow, I should say. Got it in for me.'

Sunlight came bright through the gap in the curtains to rest on the telly, and for a second the dust on the screen glowed as a great white shark swaggered out of the dark towards us.

'Don't be a copper, Eye, whatever you do.'

'As if.'

He settled back to watch telly and I did the same, but I was thinking about Trick and his family out there in the paddock.

Nine

Mum still rang every Monday night at seven o'clock on the dot and Sam still refused to answer or even be in the house at that time. There was always this awkward bit at the start of our conversation where Mum would say, 'Is Sam—?' And I would cut her off as cheerfully as I could, and rush on to a different subject. At first it made me feel bad, like the consolation prize kid, but after a while I stopped noticing.

Dad made sure he was in the Stag when she called, so I got used to settling down in his armchair in the living room and talking about things that nobody else wanted to hear about: mainly Trick Delaney.

It was funny, because when Mum actually lived here she could never listen to me. She pretended to, and thought she was pretty good at it, but I could tell when she was faking. I'd run little tests to find out, throw in funny-sounding words that I'd learned, like *scrotum* and *vestibule*, and she would nod away.

On the phone it was different. She loved hearing about the travellers, especially Trick's mum, and I told her everything I could notice. Like that all of Trick's little sisters had their ears pierced, even Ileen, the tiniest, and that sometimes in the morning before the babies were awake his mum did press-ups outside the trailer.

Matty said she wouldn't be able to take her mum leaving, but sometimes, after just a few minutes at her house with her mum, I got the urge to walk out and lie down in a field full of mud or take a swing and chuck it over the high bar in the playground so the chain twisted and nobody could play with it.

One summer, Matty pointed out that my house didn't have family photographs. Hers was like a museum: the lot of them at Disney World and dressed up in Victorian costumes and Matty every year at school.

Soon after, Mum said she couldn't afford our latest school pictures. 'We only just got the last one. You don't look any different,' she said, and she was trying to joke, but I got upset. I told her she had to get it. It would be embarrassing to be the only kid at school not buying one, and why didn't she take any pictures of us anyway? Why didn't she put some up?

'Where's this coming from?' she said. 'Why don't you ever bother your dad about this stuff?'

But the next morning she gave us money for the pictures, and a few weeks later, a collage of our last visit to Skegness appeared in the kitchen.

We didn't talk about anything like that on the phone. Instead, I told her how the two men and Trick were away from the paddock all day while Trick's mum cleaned the trailers inside and out, and how the little girls pretended to help, but mostly got in the way, and how the fire was sometimes left to go out and sometimes kept burning through the night. We spent longer on the phone every week, and I started to look forward to Monday nights.

The Monday after the break-in though, I wasn't in the mood. It was hard to be enthusiastic about the travellers with Dad walking around the way he was. He'd even let the bird feeders go empty, which was unheard of. His robin kept popping up at the kitchen window and pecking at the glass as if to say, *What did I do?*

I listened half-heartedly to Mum's description of the souks in Tunis, and the people she'd met there, and I answered Yes, and I don't know, and Probably, to her questions about whether I'd got the bracelet she'd sent, and whether Sam had read her postcard, and whether Trick was okay, until eventually she gave up and let me go.

It was hours later, when I was learning the names for wildflowers in bed, when a pounding on my door almost gave me a heart attack. Sam burst in on the third bang. In the past he would have waited, but these days he thought a warning was sufficient.

'No, *please*, come in . . .' I started, and then I saw his face.

'What does she say?' he slurred, and he put too much weight on the door handle, so it looked like it might swing away at any moment, taking him with it. His shaved head made his brown eyes look enormous.

'What?' I put my book down.

'What does she *say?*' he said, louder now. He stepped into my room, without letting go of the door. One of his eyes was closed. He stank of booze.

I didn't know what to say, and so I said, 'Not much.'

'Not much?'

'She tells me about where she's been, like Beni Khiar . . .'

'*Beni Khiar?*'

'And she asks how we are, says she loves us. That she's sorry—'

'Ha!' he said, as if that was the stupidest thing he'd heard in his life. 'And?'

'And what?'

'What does she *say*? When's she coming back? *What does she say?*'

'I . . . She didn't . . . She didn't say any of that.'

'Don't you ask her?'

I swallowed.

'You don't . . . ?' He was incredulous, and his mouth opened. He dropped his head back and made this terrible noise, the sort a baby rhinoceros might make if it had three legs broken, but was still about to charge.

His eyes glittered and he stared at me, swaying along with the door, one side of his lip raised in disgust.

'Why don't you speak to her? If you're so desperate to find out. Why don't you speak to her yourself?'

'Doesn't matter to you, does it?' he sneered. 'You don't care, do you?'

He'd let go of the door handle now, and was halfway into my room, his face a mess of rage and tears and drunkenness, and I got out of bed, ready to fight him if he wouldn't shut his mouth.

'You don't, do you?' he said. 'You've got *Dad*.'

'How would *you* know what *I* care about?'

I wished Dad would hurry up and get back from the pub.

'I hate you, Iris,' he slurred, pointing at me. 'You shouldn't talk to her. I hate you. And I hate Dad. And I hate *her* as well.'

He turned and slammed the door so hard that I felt the air sucked out from around me.

'Why don't *you* speak to her?' I shouted after him. 'If

you're so bothered! Why don't you speak to her when she rings?'

'Shut up!' he shouted, and his voice broke, and he ran upstairs.

I heard Sam throw himself down on his bed in the room above me. I got up. The door handle was still warm from where he'd been gripping it. My hands shook. I couldn't hear anything out in the hall.

He wouldn't want me; he'd tell me to go away, but I couldn't stop. I didn't knock, just pushed the door open gently.

'Get out,' he said.

He was lying exactly as I knew he would be: diagonal across his bed with his face shoved into his pillow. His Adidas Stripes had got pushed up, and I could see the ribbed ankles of his white sports socks. Their dirty soles confronted me; two sad eyes. Mum's postcard was in pieces on the floor by his bed. I'd memorised what it said.

Think of you both every day. Can't wait to see you.
Won't be long now. All my love.

I remembered coming in here when Mum and Dad were arguing. When I was small enough to climb in next to him and not care that we were squashed together.

81

There wasn't enough room, and he wouldn't budge over, and it took some effort to balance, but I made it onto the bed beside him. His breath was jagged and sad, and it hurt the piece inside me that felt just the same as it.

On the wall behind him was the outline of a king that he'd drawn in black marker pen. He'd pestered Mum and Dad to be able to do it for ages. Finally Mum had convinced Dad to let him. As long as he drew a practice picture first, and showed it to them, she said, why shouldn't kids be allowed to express themselves in their own rooms?

The king's long hair curled outwards as though he stood in the middle of a great wind. Beyond the king a medieval castle was in the process of falling down. The drawing wasn't finished.

There was a new box of pens on the floor Sam still hadn't opened. Him and Benjy both loved drawing. Benjy did these brilliant cartoons that made everyone laugh, and Sam did intricate pictures of nature and magic. He hadn't done any art stuff for weeks.

'Sorry,' I whispered, not knowing what I had to be sorry for but meaning it completely.

Sam's throat made a weird noise.

'I didn't. I didn't . . .' I stopped, not sure exactly what I didn't.

Sam lifted his arm up, and I ducked my head under,

and we lay there like that, him face down, me tucked under his arm, until the world outside disappeared, and only the drawings that covered his bedroom walls could be seen in the window.

Ten

Mum left on a weekend in the middle of May. Summer hadn't started, and it had been raining for weeks. She said she would come back. Not to Silverweed, but to Derby. She was just going away for a bit, to work things out, she said.

She'd packed the van overnight while we were sleeping.

She only took three boxes with her: one of clothes, one of cooking stuff, one of books.

'What on *earth* is the point of having all this crap?' I'd overheard her asking Tess on the phone.

I didn't understand why she'd started calling everything 'crap', like it had all just appeared one day to annoy her. Like she hadn't picked all the items herself.

Sam wanted to keep all the stuff she was leaving behind, or to put it at Tess's if it would upset Dad, but Mum wouldn't let him.

'It'll only weigh you down,' she said. 'You'll see one day.'

And all the time she spoke in this maddening, soothing way because she didn't want us to be sad about what was happening. Like that was even possible.

In the morning we had breakfast together, the three of us. Dad stayed out of the way, chopping wood. Pouring out the tea, Mum pressed her lips into a white line. She didn't look at us.

After she'd washed our plates, she crouched down and put her head against Fiasco's.

'Be a good girl now, won't you? I'll be back before you know it.'

Fiasco licked her nose.

I couldn't stop crying. I was scared we'd never see her again. She'd talked about travelling for as long as I could remember and now she was actually going. Sam just stood there and stared, and it was weird because they were the closest.

They used to mock me and Dad when we went out looking for rare insects or wildflowers. They preferred shopping and singing. It was always the two of them, making loads of noise. It had been that way since forever.

Mum had on her denim shorts and a thin beige shirt I hadn't seen before and a pair of sturdy walking sandals she'd bought from a catalogue recently. We followed her out. I stood on the drive while she looked quickly around at the yard and the flowerbeds and the pebble-dash walls of Silverweed, and I thought, *Why don't you look at* us?

Sam stayed where he was, at the midpoint of the path.

Dad put his axe down, and came to wait behind Sam. Fiasco ran up and down the path with her head low, like she was in trouble.

'I'll ring every week, and write,' Mum said. 'And as soon as I've worked out a proper plan, we'll talk about what's going to happen next. This is nothing to do with you. Remember that.'

She pulled me to her and kissed the side of my head, and told me not to worry. I was a teenager now, and I had my dad and my brother, and we were to look after each other. She said she needed to do something for herself, but she'd be back, and she'd be *happy*.

'I'm not leaving *you*, I love you,' she whispered, but it didn't make me feel better, because Dad was standing right there and she couldn't say the same to him.

She went to hold Sam but he shrank away. She looked at the ground where rain had pooled in the dips of our wonky paving stones. She nudged at the water with her toe.

'Okay,' she said. '*Okay*.'

Her van was painted sky blue, and it was the only patch of colour in the yard, and I thought that if it had been sunny she wouldn't be able to leave because it was so beautiful here then.

She opened the door and got in, and it creaked like any other car door on any other day and I wanted to jump in the back and throw her stuff out onto the drive, but instead I watched as she got the engine going, and struggled with her seatbelt, and waved very seriously, like she was taking the dog off to the vet's to be given a lethal injection. And then she went.

Sam's face was grey when I looked at him, and he was trembling, but his eyes were dry. The sound of her tyres passing over the rocks and stones on the lane was really loud for a few seconds, maybe because we were all so stunned and then Sam ran onto the lane. He ran after her for a few seconds, then stopped and picked up a stone. He threw it, and it crashed against the van. She didn't stop.

'Bitch!' he shouted.

Dad had put his arm around me at some point, and he was trying not to let me know he was crying, and it was making my breathing so uneven that my whole diaphragm got out of synch. I couldn't believe she'd done it. She'd gone. I couldn't understand what was happening.

'Breathe,' Dad said. 'That's it, breathe.' And I thought

I'd breathe a bit easier if Sam would stop acting so mental.

He crouched in the middle of the lane, his hands running over the stones like he was feeling the surface of the sea, and he had this awful expression on his face, like he didn't even know what he was doing.

I'd heard him shouting at her, the night before. The two of them had been sitting in his room, and out of nowhere I'd heard his voice.

'If you aren't leaving *us*, why can't I come? If you're *coming back*, why can't I come too?'

When his door slammed, I went to have a look, and she was just standing outside his room, staring at the door.

'*Sam*. Sam, come on, listen. Sam! Let me . . . Let me . . .' she said, but he wouldn't let her anything. He turned his music up.

She'd stared at the floor, and I could see from the way her shoulders moved that she was doing her breathing exercises. She did them every morning, cross-legged in the living room if it was raining, in the garden if it was dry. It was another one of her new things.

After she'd driven off, we drank sweet tea at the kitchen table, but it felt wrong being together. We couldn't look at each other. We ended up in our own rooms.

I re-read *The Darling Buds of May* because after a while

it always stops me from crying. Later on, Dad bought chips for tea.

The next day came, and the next week, and we went on with our lives, which were just the same except for being messier and less organised and much, much quieter.

Eleven

When I woke the morning after Sam's outburst, I had a plan. It was as clear as if I'd dreamed it. I was going to make him feel better. I rooted through the pantry. We had flour and milk. I took some change out of the dusty fruit bowl and walked to the shop with Fiasco. The sun was in the middle of burning off a layer of cloud. It was going to be another boiling day. I bought lemon, bananas, eggs and two kinds of chocolate.

I looked through our ancient cookbook, and got out all the apparatus I needed. It was still only eight o'clock so I wiped the kitchen table down and swept the floor and put the pots away. I even stood on Dad's armchair to get rid of the tomato sauce on the ceiling.

I fed Fiasco and the cats, and hit the ball as far as I could a hundred times, and then I couldn't wait any longer. I made two cups of tea and carried them upstairs.

Dad was reading in bed. 'Good girl,' he said, sitting up, surprised.

Sam was less grateful. 'What are you doing in here? Get out.'

He pulled his pillow over his head and turned over.

'Oi! I'm making pancakes. And chocolate sauce. I've been to the shop. I've got bananas and everything.'

He lifted his pillow and peered at me.

'You can't make pancakes.'

'I can.'

'What, and chocolate sauce?'

'It's easy!'

He rolled over as if he was going back to sleep, but I'd got him, I knew.

By the time Sam came down, I'd made the batter. It *was* easy, just cups of flour and milk and a couple of eggs. I don't know why I hadn't done it before. The butter had reached the perfect point. It fizzed gold, filling the kitchen with deliciousness. The thing was to get the fat really hot. Everyone knew that. I ladled the mixture in and tilted the frying pan round like Mum did. Sam sat at the kitchen table, flicking his fork between his fingers so it knocked with both ends on the wood. The chocolate melted slowly in bowls on top of the Aga.

The first pancake was perfect. I let Sam have it. He

peeled a banana halfway down, sliced it on, then spooned both types of chocolate over. He folded it in half, then half again.

He hummed while he ate it with his hands.

The next one was ready when Dad walked in. 'Pancakes? What are you after?' He moved the spoon through the batter, nodding his approval. 'Here. You have that one. I'll do mine.'

The pan hissed as Dad ladled in a new pancake. He whisked the mixture, even though I knew for a fact it was lump-free, and put the radio on.

I lemon-and-sugared my pancake. Sam shook his head at me. He had chocolate on his chin.

His scalp was so pale it was almost blue. The sun shining through the windows turned his ears coral.

'Do you like it?' I asked, pointing at his head with my fork.

Sam laughed. 'You obviously don't.'

He ducked his head, rubbing at it.

'Yeah. It feels good.'

I reached over and rubbed his scalp. It did feel pretty good, especially when you stroked the hair the wrong way.

'Punky said this would happen. Girls can't resist a skinhead.'

I pulled a face. 'Matty'll cry when she sees it.'

'Then she's an idiot. It's only hair.'

'*That's* a record!' Dad said from the Aga, after an especially impressive flip. Fiasco watched him, drooling. Sam rolled his eyes.

'Did Punky do it?'

'No, Leanne did. She loves it. She's even got her own clippers.'

'Weird.'

'I know.'

He couldn't stop touching it, and it was so strange how different he looked, just because he'd got rid of his hair.

'Jesus, Eye! It'll grow back,' he said, and I didn't even feel stupid because he'd used my nickname.

When we'd eaten more pancakes than was okay, and Dad had gone to work, I told Sam my plan.

'We're going to finish the drawing. In your room.'

'*We?*'

'Yeah. I'll help.'

He did one of those raspberry laughs, where you keep your mouth shut and let it explode through your lips. He looked out the window, like maybe he'd had something else planned.

'You've been saying you'll finish it for ages.'

'Yeah, I know but . . . I dunno. I'd like to draw *something* maybe. Don't think I'm in the mood to finish . . . *that.*'

'Oh.' I made a pattern on the table with some lemon juice.

'I don't know if I even like it any more. It's a bit . . . *shit.*'

I watched the goldcrests and blue tits on the bird table. They were all so twitchy. They never stopped turning their heads for a second. Everyone thought birds were so free but they must be the least relaxed creatures on the planet.

I realised Sam was looking at me, and tried to smile, but I was disappointed. He was just going to go meet Punky and Leanne like he always did. As if buying two types of chocolate would mean he'd stay in all day drawing with me.

'Could draw something else though,' he said. 'Go and get your bird books.'

I ran to get them, and we sat at the table, looking at birds of prey.

'This is the best one,' I said, turning to a photo of a buzzard. Sam looked at it for ages. He went upstairs to get his pencil case and his new pens.

'Okay,' he said. 'I'll draw it on your wall. But you can't annoy me.'

I didn't even promise not to in case that was annoying.

I sat on my bed, watching as he traced lines across the wall with his finger. He emptied his pencil case onto the floor. It was full of black pens with different-sized nibs. He told me to go and put his music on, loud, and leave the door open. When I got back, he was still staring at my wall. I wondered what he could see. I wasn't good at drawing. I could never get the pictures from my head onto the page.

I hugged my knees as he started sketching with a pencil. Every few minutes, he stepped back to see what he'd done. It was all circles and triangles and lines.

'There's no point putting in the detail until you know the shapes are right,' he said. 'That's where you go wrong. You do it too soon.'

It was true. I always started with the detail straight away. I couldn't resist. By the time I realised it was wrong, it was too late. My people always had wonky eyes and a squashed head.

All day, he bossed me about but I didn't mind. I changed the music when he got sick of it, and made us cups of tea and cheese toasties. He clasped and unclasped his hands sometimes to get rid of the cramp. When he was happy with his sketch, he swapped his pencil for a pen. The drawing got bigger and more detailed. Hills and trees and a stormy-looking sky appeared.

Sam pressed his lips together when he was concentrating, and it made his dimple pop. He was working on the foreground of the picture now. He had my book open, and looked at the buzzard occasionally. In its talons he drew a dead baby rabbit that wasn't from the book. The buzzard carried it through the sky.

'I love it,' I said.

He stopped what he was doing, and stepped back. He put his pen in his mouth and smiled. The plastic knocked against his teeth.

At some point I stopped worrying about being annoying and started talking. I told Sam all about Matty, and how she thought she was so incredible because she wore a bra with underwire, and he told me about how nice Leanne was, when you got to know her. I tried to believe him. I didn't say anything about Mum. I didn't want to ruin it.

When Dad and Austin got back from work, I made them come and look.

'Wow,' Austin said, brushing sawdust from his eyebrows. It was probably the most he'd said all day.

Dad whistled. He was sawdusty too. The two of them smelled of petrol and sweat and leaves.

Sam didn't stop drawing. He was finishing off the baby rabbit. Its eyes had been pecked out, and there was blood around its slack mouth. The background was a more dramatic version of the Dark Peaks. A small girl stood on a big hill staring out. Her brown curly hair blew in the wind.

'I'll never paint over it,' I said, when Sam was putting his pens away.

'You better bloody not,' he said, and he looked so happy I wanted to hug him.

Dad and Austin went back out to unload the pick-up, and I heard myself say something I hadn't been meaning to.

'I won't speak to her if you want,' I said. I spoke really quietly, and Sam looked surprised, and for a horrible second I was worried that I'd wrecked everything, but then he shook his head.

'Don't be stupid, Eye,' he said, in a gruff way that reminded me of Dad, and he zipped up his pencil case.

Twelve

By the time Wednesday arrived, when Trick had promised to do his best to sneak out, I was all mixed up. I went to the cornfield early because I couldn't wait to see him. I needed to know I was right to trust him.

Midsummer night was long gone, and the days were getting shorter, but it was still light at eight o'clock. I'd never met Trick at night-time before. Clouds high in the sky towards Ashbourne Hall were turning pink at the edges like Chinese pork, and I was hungry. Maybe we could bake some corn later. If everything was all right.

I trudged across the stepping stones, climbed through the barbed wire, and passed the ancient oak. Butterflies thrashed about in my ribcage as I walked through the green corridor. Maybe Trick would be early too. Maybe he was there right now, lying down the way he had when we first met.

But the corn den was empty.

The cushions I'd brought out for us to sit on were where we'd left them, home to a few snails by now. Their shells tapped against the dry ground as I shook them off. Woodlice skulked out from the dark, dead patches underneath. I sat down and waited. The sun sank lower.

I climbed the oak tree, identified insects and looked for dormice. I tried to remember how to make a corn dolly, and couldn't, and still Trick didn't come. I walked to the brook to see if I could spot a pike, but there were only the usual chubs and minnows, and a perch that I almost missed, hiding in the reeds.

It passed ten o'clock. Trick had said if it got this late he couldn't make it. I felt hopeless. He wasn't coming. Maybe he'd never meant to come. Why had I been so sure he wouldn't steal from us? I didn't know him at all.

I remembered his eyes, the black melty bit where his right iris drifted, and the way his hair fell across his face when he was listening to me. I *did* know him. It must be his dad. He'd found out he was hanging around with a country girl and grounded him. Or maybe he'd forgotten about me. Or realised I was an idiot.

Our harvest was shrivelling in the corner after days and days of sunshine. I picked a cob up and lobbed it at the oak tree. It was good that Trick hadn't come. I was stupid to think we could be friends. He wouldn't want to if he knew what I thought of his dad, what my family thought about *him*. That sometimes I wasn't sure myself.

The cobs at the bottom of the pile were damp and turning black, and blind grey flies crawled over them. I aimed them at the tree's middle where the trunk split into branches, until there were none left, and then I lay down. Corn stalks dug into my back and aphids landed on my arms, making me itch. The light left the sky and my arm hairs stood up.

I didn't want to go home. I would stay out here on my own until it was dark and I caught cold, and then I would go to bed for a week and eat nothing but tomato soup until someone noticed and made Mum come back and Dad cheer up, and things go back to normal.

And then the corn rustled, and my heart was light again as if I'd never felt bad at all. Trick stepped into the corn den, and he sounded as happy as I felt.

'Iris!' he cheered, and I stood up. I couldn't help it, I laughed.

He opened his arms out for a hug, and I stepped into it as though pressing the whole length of my body against his was completely normal. He smelled of soap and cigarettes and chips.

'Thought you'd have gone,' he said, giving me an extra squeeze. 'You okay?'

I nodded, but when he let go, I couldn't quite look at him.

The clouds had shifted from pink to grey, the sun had gone, but it wasn't quite dark yet.

Things felt different between us as we sat down. He was wearing his red vest, and his palest jeans, and he wore them longer than usual, rolled down to his ankles, and I wondered vaguely if that was how he always wore them at night. He was quiet, looking down at his feet tapping the warm air. Normally he started telling me things the moment he arrived, as if he'd been saving stories up for me.

'Saw the police Monday,' he said, finally.

He'd let his hair fall to cover his eyes, and it made me nervous. Why didn't he twitch it out of the way as usual? Why wouldn't he look at me?

'Tools've gone missing from the shed,' I said, and my voice sounded strangely flat and robotic.

He threw his head back and laughed. 'No way!' he said. He reached across for a corn ear, sighing.

His feet stopped tapping the air now. They knocked together occasionally instead. He pulled the leaves of the corn back to reveal the cottony strands that protected the fruit, still smiling a little.

'We thought it was starting,' he said.

I hadn't seen him at dusk before, and he looked different. The dark made his eyes look bigger or something, more sunken, and then it clicked.

'What happened to your face?' I said, and my voice sounded so dismayed it made my cheeks burn.

Trick's bottom lip disappeared under his front teeth as he bit it.

His right eyelid was puffy and had linked with the bridge of his nose to make a kind of swollen lilac eyepatch.

'Me da did it. He didn't mean to. He just pushed me. It was the way I landed. Knocked a pan off the side. It landed on me snout.'

'Is it broken?'

'The pan? Nah, it's fine. Me mammy made eggs in it this morning.'

'*Trick.*'

'Sorry. Yeah, I think it probably is.'

'Have you not been to hospital?'

'No way,' he said, quickly. 'What can they do? Break it again? I can do that meself before long. Don't worry,' he said, and he stroked my cheek with the back of his hand, and my heart beat so wild that my head swayed with the force of it.

He dug kernels out of the sweetcorn and threw them aside.

'Suppose your da thinks it was us,' Trick said.

I stuck my little finger into a deep crack in the ground. The fat little spiders came running out. We watched them dodge into different hiding places.

102

'That why he was shouting the other day?' he said.

I nodded.

'What's your brother say?'

I started babbling. I told him how many years our sheds had been undisturbed for, trying to explain.

'It's not *just* you . . .' I said.

'Oh aye. Maybe it was one of the littl'uns . . . I'm not sure what they were doing Friday night. It was probably Ileen. Now she's a *real* tinker!'

I thought of Dad watching telly with the curtains drawn, and for the first time since I'd met him I wished Trick would shut up.

'Sorry,' he said. His fair hair fell across his eyes as he looked down.

I picked a cat hair off my shorts. Trick sighed loudly.

'Where would you go anyway? If you get evicted,' I said, after a bit.

Trick shrugged. 'Me da says there's a new camp somewhere down south. Essex, I think. Me uncle bought a bit of land there. Dunno though. He never tells us nothing.'

'You'd just disappear.'

Trick lobbed a cob at the oak tree, and we watched the leaves shake as it vanished into them. I thought of Mum driving away in her sky blue van. I felt like if I stood up, I'd drag the whole earth behind me, like I weighed as much as the field we lay in.

The fingers of his other hand were spread on the crumbling soil, and I imagined putting my hand over his.

'Me mammy really likes it here as well,' he said, and he sounded so fed up that my fingers curled themselves over his without my permission. He turned his palm over, and we were holding hands, just like that.

He looked at me fiercely, and his fingers were warm between mine.

'You know none of us took nothing from your friggin' shed,' he said. 'Do you know that?'

I nodded, hoping my face looked unextraordinary because I felt such relief to hear him say it, and to know I believed him.

He lifted his hand, the one I'd been holding, and put it round my shoulder, and I leaned into him, amazed at how natural it felt. He scratched at a bit of mud on his jeans with his other hand.

'Me mammy's mad about your place, you know. She dreams of the lot of us living in there. You lot booted out.'

I laughed. 'Wish my mum was mad about it.'

Trick squeezed me. The corn shifted around us, nocturnal animals waking up.

'Sometimes, I wonder what it'd be like if she'd died instead.' It sounded terrible, even when I said it quietly. 'I mean, if we'd talk about her more.'

Trick stroked my shoulder.

'You can talk to me about her,' he said, and it wasn't the same, but it meant something that he said it. I told him how we'd talked for hours on Monday night, and then I said something I hadn't admitted to myself properly: that part of me was glad that she'd gone, glad even that Sam wouldn't speak to her, because it meant I got a look-in.

The moon had been rising for hours, and was at the top of the sky, and I shivered. Trick rubbed the goose pimples on my arms. I could just make out his swollen eyes in the moonlight.

'Tough, eh?' he said, catching me staring at his bruises. He dabbed at them.

'Maybe if it was your knuckles that were smashed up.'

He half-laughed.

'Does it hurt?'

'Nah,' he said, but when I reached out to touch it, he flinched.

'Sorry.'

I tried again.

We both watched as my hand closed in on his face. He shut his eyes, and I noticed his breathing, and mine. I thought of the word *palpitation*.

'Does that hurt?' I said, pressing my fingers light as I could against his skin.

He shook his head and swallowed, and I thought about him saying I was pretty, and what I'd said to Matty about having a boyfriend, and of all the kissing scenes I'd ever read that started just like this one. I imagined drawing my face to where his was, and putting my mouth on his, and it made my stomach flip so violently I yanked my hand away.

Trick didn't notice, or pretended not to, and we sat cross-legged the way we had all the days before, only much, much closer.

As it grew darker, Trick's face looked grainy, and my vision became less sure, but all around me buzzed and rattled and shook with life. I was aware of everything: the temperature of the breeze, the way it lifted the hairs on my arms, the distance between mine and Trick's knees.

We sat there not talking while the sky darkened, closing us in, the sides of our bodies touching, a long warm strip where we joined together.

Thirteen

I was standing in the chip shop the next time I saw Matty. It was Friday night, and Dad was leaning on the counter waiting for three cod. I'd been making a Pointillist picture of a kingfisher on the steamed-up glass when I saw something moving outside.

It was Matty. In the passenger seat of her mum's car, she waved, doing her fakest smile. They'd pulled into the spot in front of the pick-up. Donna was leaning through the gap between the seats to get her handbag from the back. If this were the old days, I would have been handing it to her.

I didn't wave, just got on with my drawing. I began building a speech bubble from the kingfisher's beak out of dots. Donna slammed the car door, and made her way towards the shop. I was at the top of the curve of the bubble now, and I could see Matty trying to look as if she didn't care what I was going to write inside it. I knew she did.

We used to do this together. When Donna was queu-ing for our chips, Matty would knock on the window to get a person's attention, and whisper instructions to me, and I would trace a heart or a kiss, or write *Piss Flaps* backwards if it was someone we hated. Someone *she* hated.

The bell rang as Donna entered, and people budged up so she could get into the packed shop. I watched Matty pretend to be interested in the houses on the oppo-site side of the road. I took my time with the bubble.

'Tommo!' Donna called. 'Tut, tut, is that your truck? Are you driving tonight then, Iris?'

Dad leaned away from the counter where he'd been examining the battered things, and grinned. I hated seeing them together. Their eyes flashed. Donna couldn't stop smiling.

'Same as usual when you're ready, Poll,' Donna called over the counter.

Poll nodded over her shoulder, shovelling chips from one compartment to another. There were spots all round her hairline even though she was old.

'Second chippy this week,' Donna fake-whispered to my dad, putting her hand to her mouth theatrically.

A chubby mother nearby rolled her eyes.

'Have you *seen* this?' Donna pushed her belly out.

'Have to get a crane round to get you out soon enough,' Dad said.

Donna pretended to hit him. It was disgusting. Her hair was a big, black curly mass, and I could just make out the smell of her hairspray and perfume over the vinegar and grease of the chips.

I turned back to the window, and caught Matty staring straight at me. I'd finished the bubble, and she was looking at me as if to say, *Get on with it then*. I imagined writing, *Your mum wants to have it off with my dad*, but *her* dad, Jacob, popped into my head.

He always brought us something nice when we were waiting for tea: a crab stick or apple slices or some crisps in a bowl. He would squeeze the backs of our heads while we were watching telly, and tell us we'd end up boss-eyed.

I settled for: Piss flaps.

'Coming to see us soon, ducky?' Donna called over to me. I wiped the window quick. 'Matty's missing you.'

Her voice changed when she talked to me, like I was a different species or something. Mum always talked to us like we were adults. Ever since I could remember she had done that.

'Suppose you're busy these days, eh?' Donna said, and she wriggled her eyebrows at me. I had no idea what she was talking about. Then I choked. Matty must have told her about Trick. I'd forgotten she even knew.

'What's that?' Dad asked, taking three forks from the box on the end of the counter.

Donna winked in my direction. I felt sick.

'Think the girls've fallen out,' she said, pouting slightly. 'Can't get anything out of Mats.'

Dad shrugged, and Donna changed the subject.

'Hear you've been invaded anyway,' she said, and for once I was relieved to hear Dad starting on about the travellers and the tool shed, and the uselessness of the police.

Poll joined in.

'Oh it'll be them all right,' she said, plonking a battered fish on top of some chips.

Her hands worked fast, wrapping up paper, putting packages into a brown bag.

'We had some near us. Moved on in the end, we got rid of them, but Jesus and the Holy Ghost. Dog shit *everywhere*. Nappies. They had a massive horse in the garden at one point. Hundreds of dogs chained up in front. Kids were bloody terrified. Had to get professionals in to sort the mess after.'

Dad held out his money, and Poll took it but didn't go to get change. She was thinking about her story. The queue was getting restless.

Dad took the package.

'Put the change in the charity box, eh Poll?' he said, looking grim.

I pushed through people to the door, keen to get out of there before Donna said anything else.

Outside, the air felt cold after the steaming chip shop, and I shivered, relief tingling down my spine. The bell dinged behind us, and my stomach settled, and we were almost inside the pick-up when a car door slammed. Matty stepped out.

'Shouldn't dump your mates first time you get a boyfriend, you know, Iris,' she called. 'You'll have no friends left when the gypsies move on.'

Dad stopped, his hand on the pick-up door handle. I squeezed the chips to me and the vinegar stung my nose.

Matty had her mouth fixed so her cheekbones were pushed upwards, her lips stretched in the worst kind of smile. I hated her.

The chip shop doorbell rang again, and Donna stepped out, brown paper package in her arms.

'What's all this?' she said, taking in mine and Matty's stand-off.

'In,' Dad barked, ignoring her.

Matty skipped off. From the car in front, she smirked back at me.

Fourteen

The journey home was silent. Dad didn't look at me. His hands fed the steering wheel left to right, his knees lifted as he switched between accelerator, clutch and brake. I felt sick.

It was cloudy for once, and getting dark outside, and Dad put his lights on. He always put them on early, not like Mum who only remembered when she saw someone else's. I leaned back against my seat, and thought about what I was going to say. That Matty had got it wrong? That Trick wasn't my boyfriend? That I'd made it up to impress her? How much difference would the all-important boyfriend distinction make to my dad?

We were on Ashbourne Road now, and the next right turn was ours. Soon it would be over, I told myself. But Dad's mouth was firm, like a decision, and I knew this was different. This wasn't getting a letter sent home for wearing trainers to school or losing the form book for the third time.

He clipped the indicator as we approached our lane and cut the engine, letting the pick-up roll home, controlling it with the brakes. We lurched in and out of potholes, and I remembered how carefully Dad used to drive when I was little and would sit on his knee, holding the wheel.

He swung onto the drive, yanking the handbrake and footbrake at the same time, and I glared at him because the seatbelt had cut into my neck, but he wouldn't look at me.

I concentrated on the patch of heat coming from the bag of chips onto my lap and belly, watching as he stared out the window. His hands gripped the steering wheel as if the whole thing might leap suddenly into the sky. The engine pinged and clicked as it cooled. Outside, a pigeon cooed.

'Come on then,' he said, and his voice was quiet. 'Let's have it.'

'What?' I said, and I sounded stupid. I knew *what*.

He turned to look at me, but it was my turn to stare out the windscreen now. A green lacewing had got splattered in the top left corner, and I noticed how the wipers kept missing it. One of its wings was pressed against the glass, and I looked at the intricate turquoise webbing.

The end of the ladder loomed over the cabin we sat in. I could see it at the top of the windscreen, and I imagined sitting up there, feeling the warm air on my cheeks, the cold metal rungs underneath me.

'Well?'

My heartbeat filled the cabin.

I opened my mouth then closed it again.

I tried to think of something that wouldn't make things worse.

'Fine.' He shouldered the door open. 'Keep your dirty secrets. You won't be seeing him again. That's for sure.'

I was shocked, and I couldn't think.

'What you waiting for? Get out. I've got to *lock* the pick-up. Don't know who you can flaming trust round here.'

He slammed his door and I jumped down, slamming my own. Dad locked up with his enormous set of keys, then jammed his hands in his pockets and stalked along the path.

The chips stank of vinegar and the dead fish that was wrapped inside, going soggy and grey. I wasn't hungry. I watched the cracked paving stones pass beneath my feet. The walk down the path took forever.

'It's not as if I had sex with him or anything,' I muttered.

He spun round.

114

'What? I didn't,' I said, louder now, because I wanted him to know he was overreacting, that nothing that bad had happened.

He moved towards me, his face screwed up, and I stepped back to get away from him. 'If that thug *dared* touch you . . .'

'He didn't,' I said, and it took all my courage to get the words out, quiet as they were. 'And he isn't a thug.'

He shook his head at me in wonder, and I pulled my shoulders back, trying to hold my head up.

'Swaggering about the place with that black eye. Have you noticed *anything* that's been going on round here?'

The chips were burning my chest, and I realised I was crushing them. I realised I was shaking my head.

'Jesus, Iris. How *thick* can you be?'

'Don't call me thick! You don't know anything about it, you're the one that's—'

'What?' he shouted, so sharply that I jumped. 'I'm the one that's *what*?' His eyes flashed, daring me to finish.

I felt my chest thudding. I swallowed. I didn't know where to start.

'He didn't do anything wrong.'

'And you know that, do you?'

I nodded.

'Because that's what he's told you?'

I wasn't daft enough to nod again.

'Know it all, don't you? And not even fourteen!'

I stared at the floor, at the silverweed growing up through a crack in the pavement. I could feel him looking at me, could hear the dislike in his voice, and I wished I could shrink down to the size of that tiny yellow flower.

'I've not lost so much as a bag of nails in fifteen years down here. That rabble move in, and within weeks there's a break-in. And you're telling me that's a coincidence? They move in, ruin a place or rob it silly, then leave it for the next bugger to clean up. Well, not me. I'm not going to be made a fool of again. I've had it! And I don't know what your lad out there's been filling your head with, but I wouldn't believe it if I were you.'

'What you going to do?' I said, and I meant to sound mature, like it didn't much matter to me, but it came out like a wail, and then the words came whining out of me again. I couldn't stop them.

'*What are you going to* do?'

Dad put his hands out, pushing the air between us away. '*What am I going to do?* It's not your *bleeding* business what I'm going to do. I'm going to do what it's my right to do. What I should have done a long time back.'

He rubbed his face, scraped his hair back from his forehead, and walked towards the kitchen.

At the door, he turned and faced me.

'Tell you one thing they have got, your lot; something sadly missing from this family. *Loyalty*.'

Fifteen

The next morning, Dad made me go to work with him. He poached eggs and toasted crumpets, and we ate in silence. Sam was still in bed. I got into the pick-up without a fuss. Austin assumed I was poorly, and let me choose the radio station. As soon as I settled on one, Dad turned it off.

They were finishing their job in the Peaks, getting rid of the last few dying elms. As soon as we arrived, I jumped from the lorry and said I was going for a walk.

Dad looked like he was about to stop me, and I stared at him, my whole face shouting, *And who do you think I'm going to meet out there?*

Austin unloaded the chainsaws, oblivious, and eventually Dad waved a hand, as if I wasn't worth bothering about. He unhooked the back end of the pick-up, let it drop, carelessly. The metal twang reverberated around the hills.

118

'Back for dinner,' he barked after me. 'Half twelve latest.'

I stamped my walking boots into the dried-out grass, trampling the pretty marsh flowers that so many other times I had stopped to identify.

He didn't have any faith in me.

We used to walk here every Saturday. If it was really sunny, Mum and Sam would come too, but generally they preferred shopping. Dad would test me on the names of trees, and I'd try to impress him with my knowledge.

'Turkey oak, defo.'

'Nah, Cecil.'

'*Turkey*. The lobes are *way* too pointy for a Cecil!'

'Could be a hybrid,' he'd say, letting me have it.

We'd stop at the White Hart and look through his pocket books about wildflowers and insects, talk about what we'd seen. He'd let me have half a pint of bitter shandy with my dinner.

Maybe I'd stop seeing Trick. It wouldn't be that hard. I'd only known him for a few weeks. I'd make up with Matty and things would go back to how they used to be. The travellers would be evicted and I'd never see Trick again. I'd forget all about him. I'd show Dad that I was loyal, that I could be trusted.

But why? When I'd done nothing wrong?

And how could I make up with Matty? She made me feel stupid just for being myself.

Dad was so certain about everything, but sometimes he didn't have a clue. I kicked at the dry floor. A cardinal beetle crept, bright red, along a piece of rotting bark. As if it could ever be inconspicuous!

I lifted my eyes, and focused straight ahead.

I would identify nothing.

Dad only liked me if I was doing what he wanted. If I was walking beside him, calling out the names of plants *he'd* taught me, I was okay, but if I was doing what *I* thought was right, he had no time for me at all. He hadn't asked me a question for months. He hadn't even listened when I told him about spotting the azure blue damselfly.

The hill was steep, and I started to run, half tripping over the frazzled tufts of grass, feeling the burn in my thighs. I filled and refilled my lungs with fresh air. I felt like I was learning something I didn't like, a hard truth, as Mum would say.

'Some people can't fit the mould that's made for them, Iris,' she'd said to me before she left. 'They get squashed in. And it's hard for them to leave, but it's harder for them to stay. They have to find other ways to be. D'you understand that?'

I'd said no, I didn't understand, because I hated it when she got like that, using annoying metaphors and talking about people who were obviously her. I'd wanted to make things harder for her, and who knows? Maybe I didn't understand then, not really.

120

From the hill's peak, I looked at the clouds that banked to the east. There was a wind building, and it blew my hair into knots. The branches of the rowan trees overhead crashed into each other, and the wind caught in my ears, howling at me. I thought about Dad down there, taking the elms down branch by branch, so sure he was right about everything, and I knew in my heart that he was wrong about this.

I made a silent promise to go and see Trick as soon as I could.

Sixteen

Whenever I got the chance, I still crept up to Dad's window to watch Trick's family. Now we were friends, I was interested in a different way. I wanted to hear how they talked to each other, and what they laughed about. I wanted to know what they said about us, the country people who were trying to get rid of them.

Trick's mum was always saying things that made him turn away, smiling, and I imagined her doing the same to me, saying things like, 'And look at you with your curly hair, a fine figure of a girl,' or pointing out that my boobs were finally growing, that I'd soon be needing to borrow one of her bras.

She was that kind of mum, I could tell. Like mine. She wanted to make people laugh.

And then one morning, when I was sitting at the table eating a cheese toastie, she walked past the kitchen window. The baby, Ileen, was wrapped in a blanket in

122

her arms. Dad was in the outside loo, which was next to the back door. He still used it sometimes, even though there'd been plumbing inside for decades.

She knocked three times, and I froze. What if she'd come to tell me to stay away from Trick? Dad was right there, behind the chipped green paint of the outside toilet door. He'd think I'd been sneaking out before I'd even had chance. I'd never be allowed out by myself again.

She knocked harder, and I opened the door.

She was even more beautiful up close. She had a freckled nose and smooth tanned skin like Trick's, but her eyes were a melting brown, and her mouth curled up at the sides, not quite in a smile.

'So sorry to bother you . . .' she said, and her voice was hoarse like Trick's, but her accent was different. Messier and more Irish. Her words crumpled into each other like kids impatient to go down a slide. They got squashed at the end.

'Who's that?' Dad called. 'Iris?'

'It's Nan Delaney . . .' she answered for me. She spoke as though this wasn't the first time they'd met, and I realised it wasn't.

'Nan De—? Hold on.'

The toilet roll holder swivelled, and I felt my cheeks burn. The chain flushed, and Dad stepped out of the loo, tucking his T-shirt into his jeans.

Nan took a step back so that she was on the path. Dad was on the doorstep, and I was behind them both, in the house. He was as thrown as I was, and I could feel him bristling.

Nan looked at Dad with hard, flat eyes, and I wondered what they'd said to each other when they'd talked before.

'I'm embarrassed to bother you, I am, but I thought it must be worth a try . . .' She let out a nervous laugh that didn't suit her. She pronounced thought as taught, like Trick. 'It's me second youngest, Patsy. The moment we've run out of water she's taken ill. Men are both at work, you see, and I can't go far because of the babies.'

She said babies to rhyme with tabbies, and can't with ant. And she wasn't here because of me.

It was obvious what she wanted, but Dad wouldn't make it easy. A look of annoyance crossed her face then disappeared just as quickly.

'I wondered if you could sell me some water, a bucket'd do. For me babby, so I can give her a bath, make her some soup . . .' She trailed off. Her green eyeliner shimmered as it caught the sunlight, and I wondered how she'd learned to apply it so perfectly.

I used to watch Mum sometimes, at the bathroom mirror. She would widen her pale blue eyes and blink onto her mascara wand. Her eyes would roll into her head for a second as she did it, then be there again,

124

staring at themselves in the mirror. She was relaxed when she did her make-up. It was like she was in a trance.

'A mother has to swallow her pride,' Nan Delaney said, and she looked at me then, as if I might understand that, and I might have, but it was too unexpected. I couldn't smile back in time, and then her bright, hard eyes were gone, gleaming again at my dad.

He breathed in slow through his nostrils, and I tensed my stomach. I couldn't bear it if he was rude when she was asking for help. I held my breath.

'You want amenities,' he said finally, 'get to a camp site.'

Nan winced, but her eyes didn't leave his. 'Easier said than done,' she said. 'Travellers not welcome at the sites these days, ruin people's holidays they say . . . Don't like us when we travel, don't like us when we stop,' she said, and I remembered Trick saying the same thing.

She reminded me so much of him. She was beautiful and tanned and freckled, but she looked hard too.

'I'm not getting into that with you. I want you gone. And you can tell your lad to stop sniffing around my daughter and all.'

He said it as an afterthought, but Nan's face changed for a second.

The sky was blue behind her, and I could hear the traffic sweeping past on Ashbourne Road, and everything seemed to slow down for a minute as she examined me, puzzling over something. When she spoke it was as though she was clapping her hands.

'Well! That's that, then!' she said. 'I'll go back to me daughter, see if I can magic her up something out of the woodwork.'

'Got me own litter to sort,' Dad said, and he turned around and walked into the house.

'*Cold* man,' Nan said, then muttered something else I couldn't make out. She took a step back, then changed her mind. Her eyes were soft again.

'Say,' she called into the kitchen, 'is the brook water right for drinking?'

Dad came back to the door. He laughed out of his nose. 'Sheep fall in. Rot, you know . . . But it's your call,' he said, shaking his head at her.

'Thank you *very* kindly!' Nan said, and she wasn't exactly polite, but as she walked off, I thought she looked dignified, with her back ironing board straight, and her baby wrapped in a blanket.

Dad filled the kettle noisily. He was trying to avoid me.

I watched from the living room window. Nan took the road round our yard to get to the paddock.

'Oh, she respects that's mine at least!' Dad called from the doorway. 'Bloody woman.'

I went into the kitchen.

'Don't start,' Dad said, before I'd even opened my mouth. 'Who goes off in the morning, and leaves four kids without water?'

'Maybe he didn't realise.'

'*Iris.*'

His beard was so bushy now, it was all wispy at the edges, and it made him look old. I wished he'd shave it off.

'I mean it, don't start. Not my fault if her husband *is* a careless pillock. And I don't trust a word she says anyway.'

'Why would she lie?'

There was amazement in Dad's eyes as he looked at me. My cheeks prickled.

'You really do believe everything everyone tells you, don't you?'

'I don't,' I said, too quickly, and the little stags were there, charging at the backs of my eyes. I blinked them away.

'You're too soft, Iris. You need to toughen up. Before you get taken for a ride, good and proper. If they've run out of water, then I'm . . .' He trailed off, searching the kitchen for inspiration.

Fiasco lifted her nose from her ball and grinned at us, her pink tongue flopping from the side of her mouth, frothy with slobber.

'Then I'm Fiasco's mother,' he said.

I didn't laugh.

'You're just saying that so you don't look bad.'

'What? I'm not Fiasco's mother?'

I opened my mouth to say something else, and he lost his temper.

'You're wrong, Iris. And I don't want to fall out with you again, so let's just leave it at that, shall we?'

The question sounded aggressive, probably because I wasn't really being asked anything, and I stared at him fiercely, but I didn't say any more.

Later that afternoon, Dad and Austin had to get some wood chippings and cement and because they needed the space in the pick-up, Dad said I could stay home. As soon as he'd gone, I ran upstairs to watch the travellers. Trick's dad's van wasn't in the paddock. The men worked all day in the week. His mum was in the caravan, and three of the little girls were doing cartwheels and handstands outside. Patsy must have been in bed. I thought of Mum, on her own, needing water somewhere.

My arms ached as I headed down the bottom field with a bucket full to the brim. It got heavier by the second, and I had to stop halfway for a rest. I tripped on a rock crossing the lane, and sent some of the water flying, but I kept going. I hadn't been in the paddock since the travellers arrived.

Dad hadn't mown the grass since Mum left. It was soft and springy under my feet. Daisies and dandelions and dock leaves crowded cow parsley and hogweed. I had to be careful not to get my foot caught in the tangles or slop water over the sides.

When I looked up, two of the little ones were sitting on the steps. A line of white washing flapped above their heads. It smelled like Trick. They stared at me, then, clutching at each other, ran up the caravan steps, calling for their mammy.

I was right by the campfire when Nan appeared.

Her face was blank as she looked at me, and I worried what she'd think about me disobeying my dad like this, but then she smiled, and her brown eyes were more lovely than ever. The breeze caught her long red hair as she walked, lifting it behind her, the sunlight turning it fiery.

Her nails were painted turquoise, and I could see the way her hair curled on the back of her neck, just like Mum's did, and I knew exactly how it would feel if I touched it: warm and silky and soft. I handed the water over, careful not to spill any. She smelled of raspberries, and washing powder and, ever so faintly, smoke.

My skeleton felt like chocolate mousse, and I hoped that she would say something quick because words had escaped me forever.

Gold bracelets on her arm jangled against her narrow

wrist as she took the bucket. She cocked her head to one side.

'You're a kind girl,' she said, and she put her empty hand out and squeezed my shoulder. 'A good girl, I think. So don't you be telling our Patrick I've been up to see you. He won't like that. Proud like his daddy that boy . . .'

I shook my head. I tried to think of something to say.

'Come to think of it, you'd better be getting back before *any*body sees.'

She turned and carried the water towards her caravan, and I stood mute, my shoulder tingling where her hand had been.

The girls had come to the bottom of the steps at some point, and had their hands in front of their mouths, giggling, and the noise of their laughter snapped me out of it, and sent me running back towards Silverweed.

Seventeen

Dad had gone back to playing Mum's music. In the daytime, when he was working or doing stuff around the house, he had a lovely voice, but at night when he'd been drinking it got all broken and raspy.

He sang 'These Arms of Mine' and 'Stand By Me' and I knew he was going through the CDs she'd left in a shoebox by the telly, the ones she used to play when he was at the pub. I twisted loo roll into my ears, and put my head under the duvet, but the tissue fell out and under the covers got all hot and sweaty, and I couldn't shake the feeling that I was living in some kind of damaged animal shelter instead of a loving family home. It took a long time to get to sleep.

That night, Dad was watching nature programmes in the living room, making his way through a four-pack. This was his new habit. Instead of going to The Stag, he watched telly until he was drunk enough to play Mum's music. Sometimes I watched stuff with him, but mostly I read in my room. He looked too sad when he drank.

My eyes felt scratchy from lack of sleep as I made us both hot chocolate. Taking a mug, he almost smiled at me, then remembered how I'd disappointed him. I saw it on his face.

I drank my chocolate quickly, then took myself off to my room.

I lay on the bed with my book, but couldn't concentrate on reading. I'd microwaved the hot chocolate too long, and it had burned my mouth. There was a mosquito in the room and it kept shrieking past my ear. I was never going to get to sleep. My twisted toilet roll earplugs waited on my bedside table. I kept looking out the window. Was Trick in the corn den waiting for me right now? My room was on the ground floor. It would be so easy to open the window and climb out.

The mosquito screeched by again, and I jumped up to hunt it, but it had disappeared. The opening bars of 'Stand By Me' came out of the living room, and I couldn't take it. I was on my desk, out the window and in the front garden before I'd even decided.

A breeze blew the rose bush outside my bedroom window as I crouched on the ground there, listening. It was almost eleven, and I was so glad I didn't have to listen to Dad's broken singing, but guilt was like a little animal curled up in my stomach.

132

I couldn't get to the paddock without passing the side of the house where Dad was, and the moon meant it wasn't quite dark enough to make a run for it safely. If he stood up for any reason or looked out the window, he'd see me in a second.

The grass was cool against my fingertips as I made my way along the front of the house, spider-like. It was about ten metres from the end of my window to the living room. Twelve of these strange spindly steps should do it. I counted them to keep calm. The daisies had closed their heads for the night, and the air was sweet with grass and roses, but Dad was singing in the room just behind me and it made my stomach ache. The living room windows were wide open, and I heard Dad crush an empty can and chuck it in the log box. I took a deep breath. I imagined Trick, in his red vest and faded jeans, waiting for me, and I ran.

Wind filled my ears and my heart thumped away, and every second that passed I expected to hear Dad shouting from the window, but it didn't come, and so I kept going, using my arms properly the way I never bothered to in PE, no matter what Mr Limb said. I dodged potholes with man-sized strides, took balletic leaps, pointed my toes, and then I was at the pig farmer's gate, up and over, and running again, not needing to any more, but wanting to, because I'd done it! I had escaped from the house, and I was going to see Trick.

Eighteen

The corn den was empty.

I rested my hands on my thighs, tried to get my breath back. My legs were scratched from the corn and brambles and nettles I'd run through. I swore, and then something hit me on the head.

'Thought you were a goner.'

I spun round. Trick was in the oak tree. A baby acorn landed near my feet.

'I am,' I said, thinking what would happen if Dad checked my room.

I dug my foot into a hollow in the trunk, pulled myself up using the lowest branch.

'Hey! I put a nail in for you.'

I looked down at the trunk. A shiny nail stuck out.

'Bought it specially!'

'I'm too good,' I said, looping my arms around the next branch and heaving myself up.

'Hammered my thumb and everything,' he lied, holding up two perfect thumbs for examination. His hair fell across his eye, which was less swollen now. He wiped it back off his forehead.

I stood in the tree's fork, leaning against the trunk. He was wearing a white vest tonight, instead of his usual red one, and his jeans were long, and then I realised. He'd fitted a pair of cinema seats into the place where the trunk split into three.

He laughed, and started talking really fast.

'Got 'em from the tip! Me da said I could have 'em, I didn't tell him what for, mind, or he'd have my head for a souvenir. I've been desperate for you to come down and see. Look, brackets and everything.'

'Brilliant,' I said.

He patted the seat next to him. It was velvet. 'Got another surprise for you as well. I'm so glad you're here . . .'

He talked on about what else they'd found at the tip, and he was so excited, but I was finding it hard to listen.

Through the leaves of the oak tree, in the moonlight, I could see the wispy flowers waving above the maize crop, and the rows that it grew in, which were never clear when you were standing in them. I could see the tall trees that edged the brook, and the travellers' caravans, and the hawthorn hedge that surrounded the lane, and our yard, and the pick-up.

'Where've you been?' Trick asked, nudging my shoulder with his, and I made an exhausted sound with my mouth.

I told him all about it: that Matty had told on me, and Dad was hardly talking to me, that Sam was out all the time. It wasn't until I got to the bit about his mum asking for water that he spoke.

'She came to the house? Christ! She makes things worse. What'd your da say?'

'He didn't believe her.'

Trick smiled grimly, looking down at our feet. 'Who would? As if we'd leave her on her own, without any water.'

I thought of myself lugging the bucket of water down there, and wondered if it was possible for a human head to explode from embarrassment.

'He's not been to the pub since he found out. He stayed in all weekend. He's keeping watch.'

'Not very well,' Trick said, but I couldn't laugh.

Blue light came from our living room, and I thought of Dad inside, watching telly on his own. He was right. I was too soft. I was stupid to trust everybody.

'Hey,' he said. 'I didn't mean it.'

I held my breath, and tipped my head back, blinking at the branches above.

'I shouldn't have come out here. I didn't mean to. I just wanted . . . I wanted to tell you . . . Oh, I don't know.'

Trick put his arm round me. He used the crook of his finger to dry under my eyes. I wiped my nose on the bottom of my T-shirt.

He got up from his seat, and jumped into the cornfield.

'Come on!' he called, impatiently.

'What? Where are we going?'

'Exactly, Iris! Where *are* we going? It's so mysterious. Let's see.'

He held his hands out to help me down, and I ignored them as usual, jumping from the lowest branch to land knees bent on the tangle of weeds below.

He started running, and I thought back to the first time we'd met, when he showed me this place.

We ran all the way along the brook to the furthest edge of the cornfield, past the meadow and Drum Hill, into the Ashbourne Estate.

The lake was black and silver in the moonlight. The sky was so clear we could see the Milky Way.

Trick grabbed my hand, and pulled me along the water's edge to the ancient oaks. He stopped at a mess of holly and brambles, and leaned into it, swearing as he got scratched. He dragged out a wooden rowing boat.

In the daytime you could rent them. Families and couples rowed to the island in the middle of the lake. I'd never done it before because the park ranger had chased us so many times for sneaking in that we had to stay out of his way.

'I freed one for you,' Trick said.

We took our flip-flops off, and Trick rolled up his jeans and we walked the little boat into the water.

It was cool and lovely, and the noise of it made me need a wee. Cold mud slipped between my toes.

'Ladies first,' he said, and I rolled my eyes at him, and climbed in. He jumped in after me, and the boat slapped against the water. I put the oars into the rowlocks and started rowing.

He was quiet as we floated away from the bank. We looked at the sky. There were no clouds anywhere. The moon reflected in the black surface of the lake. Trick trailed his hand in the water. The oars splashed out a rhythm.

'My go,' he said after a while, but I didn't want to stop. I liked the way it felt, how I had to focus all my attention on getting the rhythm right. My arms ached, and I worked them harder.

'Fine,' he said.

He stood up, rocking the boat as much as he could. I tried to keep rowing, but it was impossible. I flicked water at him with an oar.

'You'll pay for that,' he said.

He pulled his vest off, and I saw how thin he was. He didn't even have to unbutton his jeans to take them off.

138

He just slid them down. He smiled at me, and his wonky eyes flashed, and I felt the need to examine a sycamore leaf floating by on the water.

'Seeya!' he said, and he half somersaulted off the boat.

He came up gasping and frantic.

'Water's lovely!' he said. He did a thrashy front crawl, as fast as he could.

He came to the side of the boat and prepared to splash me, but I screwed up my face at him, and stood. Without taking anything off, I jumped.

It was as freezing as ever and we raced each other to keep warm. We tried to touch the bottom and floated on our backs. Trick tried to scare me, shouting that things were biting him, and I pretended to be scare-proof which in the black water wasn't easy, and then just before we dropped to the temperature of the lake, we climbed back into the boat. The summer air dried us off as I headed to the island.

A family of ducks quacked a warning to each other as we approached, and we heard something drop into the black water. I used the oars to pull alongside the island. Willows made a sort of shelter above our heads. Trick came to sit beside me.

He nudged me with his shoulder.

'You know, you're the best girl I've ever known, Iris. Hands down. You can do everything.'

139

My heart spun like a Catherine wheel, and I wanted to tell him he was the best boy I'd ever known, that I wished that he could stay in our paddock forever, and I was desperate to touch him, just to put my arm around his back, but I couldn't do it. I just sat there listening to my heart and the night, and waiting, until gradually, the air grew stiller, and it felt less like bats swarming.

Blackbirds nested somewhere above us. I heard their warning call, and looked up to see if I could spot them.

'What you thinking?' Trick said, and his voice was very soft and very low.

'Blackbird,' I said, automatically. 'Listen.'

I held a finger up, as if that's what I'd been doing all along, as if that was what I was interested in. I thought of Dad at teatime, flicking through his book about wild-flowers as if there was nothing else important in the world, and Mum in her sky blue van driving away from everything that mattered, and it was like my body was daring me to do something that my mind hadn't agreed to yet.

I turned my head, and there he was waiting for me, his eyes still grey though I couldn't tell it in the dark, his irises still odd, and he smelled of cigarettes and chewing gum and chips, and it was lovely, and when I put my mouth against his and kissed him, it was as if I'd always known how to kiss, and how stupid it was, how unbe-lievably stupid that I could have worried about *this*.

140

Nineteen

I went back into the house through the kitchen. Dad's room was above mine, and I didn't want him to hear me climbing through the window. It was darker inside than out, but as soon as I crept in, I heard someone. I froze, widening my eyes to see better. Dad was sitting at the table. My heart ram-raided my chest.

But Dad would be standing up, switching the light on, shouting.

It was Sam. And he had his head in his hands.

'What's up?' I whispered.

'Piss off,' he said, but he didn't sound angry.

He sniffed, palms jammed into his eye sockets.

I sat in Dad's chair, next to him.

'What's happened?'

He rubbed his eyes, and breathed in sharply. I switched on the lamp by the phone.

There was a thin trail of dappled black blood running

from his nose to his top lip. Both nostrils were edged with it. His left eye was beginning to close.

I filled a mixing bowl with warm water and put it on the table. The tea towels were greasy and smelled bad, so I dunked the bottom of my T-shirt instead.

'*Careful*,' Sam said, as I dabbed his face.

'Shhhh! Dad'll be down.' I wrung my T-shirt over the bowl, sending the water pink, and started again, gently as I could.

'Who've you been fighting this time?'

He shook his head.

The room was quiet except for the trickling of water.

'I nearly had them,' Sam said, after a while.

'Looks like it.'

'You didn't see. There were two of them. They were loads bigger than me.'

In the living room, Fiasco changed position and exhaled from her nose.

'You don't always have to fight, you know.'

'That what your boyfriend says?'

I stared at him.

'Cause he's a liar if he does.'

I stopped cleaning his face, and took the bowl to the sink.

'That where you've been?' he said.

I poured the pink water down the plughole.

'I know anyway,' he said. 'It's obvious.'

'Why ask then?'

'You want to watch him, you know, Iris.'

My heart was beating fast, and I rinsed the bowl, so he couldn't see my face.

'Got chucked out his last school for battering someone, you know.'

I relaxed. 'Oh, I know about that.'

'He put them in hospital.'

'It wasn't his fault.'

Sam didn't say anything, but I could tell what he was thinking: that I was a little idiot.

The clock ticked between us and the tap dripped.

'You won't say anything though, will you?' I said.

He looked at his knuckles, which were swollen and raw, for so long I thought he'd forgotten I'd asked him a question.

'Course I won't,' he said, and the way he said it made me feel bad for asking.

His skinhead was growing out, and it was at that fluffy stage, like a kitten's fur, or a scuffed-up tennis ball, not the look he was going for at all.

'Your head looks like an old tennis ball.'

'You can talk. Do you even know you've got a stick in your hair?'

I glared at him, but his eyes were teasing.

'Gypo,' he said, and I threw the stick at his face.

143

'They're not even gypsies. You don't know what you're on about.'

'Pikeys, then. Tinkers. Whatever.'

I rolled my eyes.

'Whatever they are, they'd best be clearing off soon.'

He screwed his face up as he talked, all sign of teasing gone, and with his left eye almost shut and his lip swollen he looked like a stranger. He kept touching his face, as if it was unfamiliar to him as well, and I felt like asking him who he was and what he was doing in our kitchen.

But I didn't. Instead, I asked him again what had happened.

He looked at me, considering.

'Hardly gonna tell, am I?' I said.

He was nervous, but I could tell he was desperate to talk about it, so I just waited, like Trick would.

'Promise you'll keep your mouth shut, Eye. I mean it.'

'When have I ever *not* kept my mouth shut?'

'Yeah, but this is bad,' he said.

His voice was the lowest whisper, and I leaned forward to hear him, pushing my hair behind my ears as if that would make a difference.

'Punky cut someone,' he said. 'I knew summat was up soon as he came out. He didn't even say hello, just had his head between his knees making a spit puddle.

144

He gets like that sometimes. He wouldn't even talk to Leanne. She was sitting right next to him, kissing him and that, but he just ignored her.

'Then the bus came and these lads got off, all dressed up from town, and he was like, "Nice shirts! You go shopping for them together?" Calling them gay and that, and they just ignored him, but he wouldn't leave it. He started calling them rude for not answering, and one of them near the back turned around, and Punky just headbutted him.'

I nodded my head for him to go on. His left foot juddered against the floor as he talked.

'He'd only been out ten minutes and there was a rumble. It was five against three. People came out of the chippy, shouting that we'd best stop, that they'd called the police, but nobody actually did owt. I got a couple of good hits in, but then another one started on me, and I ended up on the floor taking a right battering.

'I couldn't do anything, just had to lie there protecting my head. I thought I was never gonna get up, and I was so winded, I couldn't get a breath, and I'd left my inhaler at home, and then it finishes. Just like that. And I look up, through my fingers, thinking it's the pigs, but it's just Punky. He's standing over me, and the townies are silent because in his hand he's got a knife.'

He looked at me, and I made my face blank because I didn't want him to stop talking.

'It was only a Stanley knife, but with the blade yoiked up it looked bad, and the townies start moving backwards. The people outside the chippy were still shouting about the police, but Punky didn't care.

'He was grinning at them, daring them to kick me now, and I was on my feet. They couldn't speak! And then for some reason, God knows why, the one who got headbutted in the first place just lurched at the knife, and Punky lunged too, and it cut right through that bit of skin.'

He pulled at the bit of skin between his thumb and forefinger, and I shivered. I couldn't help it.

I squeezed my eyes shut for a second.

'Oh my God.'

'I know. The weird thing was, the towny didn't even shout. His face went green, and blood spurted out all over his chinos.'

There was a long silence where we looked at each other.

'And *you're* telling *me* to be careful?' I said.

Sam tried to laugh, but he looked frightened. He looked excited too. His eyes flashed in the lamplight. 'He's never done it before. He couldn't believe it. That's all he kept saying at the rec. "I cut someone. I can't believe I actually cut someone."'

We sat at the table for a long time after that, and Sam made us both Horlicks, but it wasn't comforting at all.

Twenty

Dad's friend Fraz arrived on his pushbike Thursday evening. I didn't want to talk to him, but I couldn't help staring. He looked so different. He had a big red beard now, but you could still see his scars, creeping from the fuzz of it, reaching for his eye.

'Blasted thing,' Fraz said, getting off his bike. He kicked it so hard it flipped into the ditch.

Whenever I saw him I thought of his ex-wife, Mandy. He'd brought her round to meet Mum and Dad the day after he'd married her. She wore tight jeans under her biker leathers, and her head wobbled when she talked. Mum made spaghetti bolognese for tea, and interrogated Mandy. The four of them were at the kitchen table drinking when me and Sam had to go to bed.

I woke to hear the living room being pulled apart. When we got to the kitchen, Fraz was pulling Mandy out the door by her hair. Dad was trying to get him off her. Mum screamed at us to get back to bed. She shut the kitchen door on us, but we stayed on the stairs, listening. They managed to lock Fraz outside, and he shouted abuse at them until the police came and took him to the cells.

Mandy was still there at breakfast, make-up round her eyes. Her head wobbled as she stared at her scrambled eggs, and Mum tried to talk through her options.

We never really found out what happened, and we never saw Mandy again, but the day after, Fraz crashed his motorbike. Everyone said he was lucky to be alive. The motorway ripped the skin from his right hand to his right ear, and his leg was shattered.

Dad wanted to visit him in hospital, but Mum was angry. Why did he want to go and see that wife-beater? Why did he even have friends like that? Dad said he'd known Fraz since the first day of school, and that meant something, but Mum didn't care. She said Fraz wasn't allowed in the house any more.

In the end, Dad visited. He was the only person not family to make the effort. Fraz went on about it every time he came round afterwards.

'My truest friend,' he'd bellow, squeezing Dad around his neck so hard he dipped his head. Mum would bang around upstairs until him and Dad went out, fishing or to the pub.

Fraz hadn't been able to get back on his motorbike since. His hands shook so much he couldn't squeeze the handlebars. Now he went everywhere on this battered pushbike. He left it upside down in the ditch while he came into the house.

I made cups of tea and threw the ball for Fiasco. I wanted to know what Fraz was doing here. He kept Dad's glass topped up with whisky, and they changed the subject every time I walked in, but it was obvious they were on about the travellers. I hated Dad for not trusting me, until I realised he had a point. Because what was I spying on him for anyway?

Fraz took a joint from behind his good ear, and lit it while Dad talked about Sam. He hadn't fallen for his story about getting jumped outside the chippy – especially since Poll had rung up with a quite different version of events – and when he'd demanded the truth, Sam had threatened to move out.

'"*Please*," I said, "try it,"' Dad said. ' "It'd save me a fortune in crisps."'

Fraz laughed his smoked-out laugh, and you could just make out his red, shiny lips between his moustache and beard.

I was surprised to hear Dad joking about the fight with Sam. I'd gone to see what all the racket was about this morning and found them arguing in the kitchen,

Fiasco barking at their feet. Sam had said he hated living here, that he'd rather live anywhere else. He'd said it was a shithole, and I'd thought Dad was going to grab him, or throw something, but he just stood there, breathing very slowly. He closed his eyes.

It had confused Sam so much that he'd actually shut up. He slipped past me, upstairs to his room. He didn't even turn his music on.

'It'll end in tears,' Dad said now, smoke in his words.

Fraz left long after midnight, after Dad had fallen asleep at the table. Fag ends floated in whisky, and the whole kitchen stank. I emptied them out, and opened the windows. I got Dad a pint of water.

'Sorry, Eye,' he mumbled, as he walked unsteadily to his room.

I lay on my bed and stared at the picture Sam had drawn on my wall for a long time. It was his best yet. The sky was cloudy and dark, and the landscape looked mean. The rabbit's entrails dripped onto the hills.

Twenty-one

The next night I snuck out to see Trick, but I couldn't relax. I kept thinking about Sam's bruises, and Punky's knife. It was raining for the first time in ages and we sat underneath the cricket pavilion, listening to it, and leaning against each other for warmth. We'd started off at the cinema seats, but rain had created a drip system through the leaves, and seeing as we were getting almost as wet as if we were lying on the ground, we decided to find shelter.

The white paint on the posts was flaking, and I picked out the shape of a heart, then turned it into a balloon with a long string before Trick noticed. The rain let up, and we talked about moving, but stayed huddled where we were. Seagulls circled, pale against the navy sky, and clouds like bandages moved slowly across the fat moon. Somewhere nearby a can rattled across the ground.

152

My fingernails had grown long without me noticing, and I bit an edge, thinking about Sam and Dad, and Fraz with all his scars. Trick was telling me about something that had happened on their scrap rounds, and I knew from his tone that it was meant to be funny, so I laughed.

'You all right?' he said, and he sounded doubtful, so I nodded enthusiastically.

He narrowed his eyes at me. His hair was damp from the rain and it clumped together on his forehead.

'Not seen you gnawing at your claws like that before.'

'I used to bite them really bad. My hands looked like an alien's.'

I peeled off the top of my thumbnail, leaving a raggedy edge. I spat it out.

'Kinda gross actually,' he said.

The tin can moved again nearby, scraping itself across the wet ground, and I wondered what Trick would say if I told him about my brother, and Punky's knife, and then there was a whizzing sound, and a rocket shot into the sky.

We watched it explode. The green light turned to smoke and we heard laughing. Sam and a boy I'd never seen before bowled through the gate to the cricket pitch and started sticking fireworks into the lawn. Leanne and Punky were behind them, arms around each other, smoking. All the boys' heads were

153

shaved. The one I hadn't seen before wore a black wool hat.

They stopped to watch the fireworks, their faces shifting around in the flare of them. They laughed at how they tore out of the grass, leaving a messy skid mark. The smell of gunpowder mixed with the rain.

I felt Trick tense beside me.

The pit bull noticed us first. It growled and began to bark, its hind legs lifting with the force of it. Its teeth flashed as it opened its enormous head, and the group looked our way.

'Eh up, kiddies,' Punky called.

Leanne giggled. 'Hiya, girls!'

Both of them wore tracky bottoms with black jumpers. White T-shirts poked out the middle like a frill.

'Hell you doing out here?' Sam said, walking towards us. I couldn't tell if he was scared or angry.

'Don't be nasty to your little sister!'

'Shut up, Punky,' Sam said.

Trick had moved away, so our knees were no longer touching, and I missed the warmth. I wished Sam would stop staring at him the way he was.

'What did I say to you?' he said, and I was about to answer that he hadn't said anything to me when I realised he was talking to Trick.

Trick looked like he hated my brother. I didn't even know they'd spoken to each other. It hadn't crossed my

154

mind. He eased himself to a standing position, and I stood next to him, back straight to get my full height though it wasn't much. Trick's arms hung at his sides, and I wished he would wrap one around me, like Punky did Leanne.

Sam's knuckles were clenched.

'Iris, what you doing out here with him? It's the middle of the night.'

I stared at him, annoyed by the way he was talking to me, like he was my boss or something and I had to do whatever he said. As if he always talked to me like this.

'We were just going,' Trick said, holding his palms out.

'I'm talking to my sister,' Sam said, not looking at Trick.

'Hear that, Pikelet? He wasn't talking to you.' Punky spoke with a perfect Irish accent, one much cleaner than Trick's. He took a step towards us, smirking, and spat on the floor.

'You don't scare me, fella,' Trick said, and I could hear the smile in his voice.

The boy with the wool hat spoke lazily. 'Scare you if he sliced you up a bit?'

He looked like he didn't care what happened to him or anyone, like if you asked him what he was doing out here he wouldn't even know.

'Now that would be unnecessary,' Trick said. 'Seeing as how we were just leaving, peaceful, and of our own accord.'

Sam was acting really strange. He kept looking in my direction with this odd expression, and he couldn't keep still. His nostrils curled like we smelled bad to him, and I stared and stared at him, but he wouldn't look at me properly. He looked wrong out here with his shaved head. He wasn't like Punky. He wasn't even like Trick. He was faking, and he knew that I could tell. He hated it.

Punky moved closer, and I could smell his deodorant and sweat, and the faint smell of dog under the fag smoke and beer.

'Your brother don't like your mate, Iris,' Punky said. 'He wants your mate to get his scrounging arse out of here.'

'He will soon,' Sam laughed. 'My dad's gonna use a tractor to tow his mum and sisters away.'

Trick shot a glance at me, and my heart exploded.

'Try it,' he said. 'Find out what you're dealing with. Come on, Iris.'

He started walking off, and I followed, desperate to get out of there.

'What d'you bring her out here for anyway?' Punky called after us. 'Want to have a go on her in private, did you?'

I couldn't help looking back, but Trick kept on walking.

'Ah, just shut up, would yer?' he called over his shoulder.

'She's not even fourteen, Punky,' I heard Sam say. '*Jesus.*'

The whole time we walked from the cricket ground I expected footsteps to charge at us, or a can to smack us on the back of the head, but I marched beside Trick anyway, and I didn't look back again, and with every step I saw how easy it was to get used to acting like you weren't scared of anything.

'Gypos not welcome,' Punky bellowed, far behind us now, and there was Leanne's laugh, high-pitched and fun-sounding, like a kid's party, and a rocket fizzed into the sky.

'Nice mates, your brother's got,' Trick said when we were back on Memorial Lane.

I thought of Benjy with his floppy hair, sitting with Sam by the brook, threading maggots onto a fishing hook.

'They're not his mates . . .'

Trick laughed out his nose.

'They're not.'

I stopped walking, but Trick didn't.

'He isn't really like this . . .' I said, and I wondered if I was telling Trick or myself.

'He isn't. Wait!'

Trick slowed down then. He let me catch up.

'It's since Mum left. He won't talk about it. He gets so angry. He's just . . . He isn't really like this.'

The way Trick was looking at me made me shut up. His eyes were soft, and his head was tilted, and I didn't understand.

I looked ahead, towards the house. The kitchen light was on, and I felt like crying. I was remembering how Mum had tried to hold Sam but he hadn't let her, and how she'd just said, 'Okay,' because that was her big thing: respecting our feelings, *giving them room*, and I was thinking how maybe that was a pretty stupid idea. I was thinking too that maybe I shouldn't be making excuses for my brother.

I walked right past my house, and I didn't even watch to make sure Dad didn't see. I didn't care. Everything felt different, and I didn't want to leave Trick. I didn't want things to change.

We got to the entrance to the paddock and stopped.

'What are you doing, Iris?' Trick said.

I didn't know. I couldn't go any further; the trailers were right there, but I couldn't go home either, and I knew I was talking to the wrong person, but I couldn't stop.

'I'm worried about him, Trick. That wasn't him out there. And Punky . . .'

I couldn't get the words out.

'Punky cut someone,' I said, and Trick shook his head while I told him what had happened outside the chippy.

'I promised not to say anything.'

Trick was so angry I wished I'd kept my mouth shut.

'Christ! They'll end up in prison. Probably for murdering me. That Punky's bad enough without a knife. And your brother'll do anything he says.'

'He wouldn't. You don't know anything about him.'

Trick's body was in shadow, but his face was patterned with the moonlight that shone through the branches nearby.

'You're right.' He held his hands out and half laughed. 'I don't. And I'm not sorry, to be honest with you.'

He took another step backwards, closer to the camp.

I stayed where I was, on the road.

'I'm sorry we're not on the same side, Iris,' he said, without lowering his voice, and then he turned, and I listened to his flip-flops crush the long grass as he walked to his caravan.

In the trees, a pair of owls called to each other, finishing off each other's sentences so perfectly it was hard to tell where one ended and the other began.

I watched Trick go, and I wanted so much to call after him, but I had no idea what to say.

Twenty-two

The smell of garlic and onions filled the house. I sat in the kitchen listening to the radio while Dad chopped mushrooms and peppers, and opened tins of sweetcorn and pineapple. The mince sizzled away. Dad had invented his own version of lasagne. It was amazing.

Every now and then, he'd bang a utensil down and exclaim something.

'That mad little bastard! I told Sam to stay away!'

First thing this morning, WPC Baker had rung. Punky, Sam, Dean and Leanne had been seen running out of our road the night the shed was broken into. Punky had been caught smashing a fence with a stretch of chain the night after. When I'd got up this morning, Dad had been hiding all of Sam's trainers.

'He won't dare go out without shoes,' he'd told me, taking a black bin liner of them out to the pick-up. 'Not brave enough. That's his problem. Was as a littl'un.

160

Used to terrify your mum. She'd find him just about to step out of a first-floor window, or winded in a heap at the bottom of the stairs. The whole thirteen he used to jump. Absolutely fearless.'

His expression had changed then, and he'd remembered me.

'I don't know what to do with him, Iris. I don't.'

All day my heart had felt like it was being pulled down by something, maybe by my large intestine. Like they'd been dancing together in the night and gotten all tangled up. Everything was a mess. Everything had always been a mess – but I was suddenly aware of it. Sam and his friends had broken into the tool shed. They'd threatened Trick.

It was still light outside, just, and air blew in through the open windows and door. It smelled sweet, like drying hay and manure and mown lawns, and I tried to imagine we were just a regular family preparing for dinner. I tried to remember how that felt.

Any bad feeling left over between me and Dad disappeared under what Sam had done. We tried to joke around as if it were the old days, but my stomach churned the whole time. Dad was trying too hard, and my laugh sounded mental.

When the food was nearly ready, Dad told me to go and call my brother. I didn't want to talk to him, but I did as I was told. I didn't want to make things in the house any worse.

Sam hadn't been down all day, and his room was quiet. Dad had told him to turn his music off for once. He didn't answer when I shouted from the bottom of the stairs, and I was scared suddenly. He wasn't even in there! He'd sneaked out. And Dad was slaving away over that stupid dinner. I walked up the stairs and called him again. Dad was going to go mad. I knocked on his bedroom door.

'Sam?'

I pushed it open. His room was immaculate as ever, except for him, lying on his back on the floor with his headphones on, eyes closed, smoking.

I nudged him with my foot, and he looked at me.

'Out,' he monotoned, without lifting his head.

A small bottle of vodka sat next to him.

I turned the music down.

'Tea's ready,' I said, as evenly as I could.

He reached for the vodka, but I was too quick.

'No way,' I said, shoving it in the back of my waist-band. There were a few centimetres left in the bottle.

'Iris . . .' he said half-heartedly. He took his head-phones off and stared at me miserably. My anger disappeared.

'He's making lasagne, Sam. It's taken him ages. He's done proper garlic bread and everything.'

'Not hungry,' he said, dropping his head onto the floor.

'Wait,' I said, even though he clearly wasn't going

162

anywhere. I ran downstairs, hid the vodka in my room and filled an old tea mug with water. I took it back upstairs and held it out to him.

'Drink,' I ordered, out of breath from running.

He didn't move.

'D'you want Dad to come up? Because he will. He's gonna *make* you eat this lasagne.'

'Jesus, Iris! Just shut up a minute! Close the door.'

I didn't close the door until he'd taken a swig from the mug.

I sat on his bed. It smelled of feet and deodorant. The whole room did. Every now and then his curtains blew into the room with the breeze.

'Don't look at me like that,' he said, dipping his finger into the mug to catch something.

I couldn't wait for his hair to grow back. I hated looking at his fuzzy head. He took a long drag on his fag. I watched the tobacco blaze.

'I mean it. Don't look at me like that.'

He was slipping into his hard act. He changed his style of smoking, doing it the special way, where he put the filter to one side of his mouth and cupped the tip with his palm. He narrowed his eyes as he inhaled.

'You're not very convincing, you know,' I said.

He blew a perfect smoke ring.

'New trick,' I said. '*Wow.*'

'*Wow,*' he mocked.

His cigarette had burned down to the filter, and was starting to smell toxic. I snatched it from his mouth and threw it out the window. We stared at each other, angrily, and then he laughed. I joined in, I couldn't help it.

I looked at the king on the wall behind him. His arm pointed left, out the window in the direction of where the travellers were, and I imagined Trick curled up on the sofa watching telly, or eating his tea round their tiny kitchen table.

'D'you really think it's shit?' I asked.

I reached over to trace the outline of a perfectly drawn vine with my finger. The wall was smooth and cold.

'I think you should finish it,' I said.

Sam laughed in that way that isn't a laugh.

'What's the point? No one cares if you can draw a perfect replica of a medieval castle.'

'I do,' I said, and the words floated between us, simple and true.

He sighed. 'Please will you stop looking at me like that, Eye?'

'I just don't understand. Why can't you just make friends with Benjy?'

'Why don't *you* make friends with Matty? Not seen her for a bit.'

'That's different. Matty got me in trouble. Dad's only just started talking to me again.'

'Yeah, well. Benjy's a baby. He still thinks he's gonna get scouted for England and he can't even tackle!'

He'd sat up now, and crossed his legs, and I could smell the alcohol coming off him. I made him drink the last of the water.

'He doesn't know anything,' Sam said.

'He knows loads of stuff. What d'you mean?'

Sam shrugged. 'Nothing's ever happened to him. Punky's dad got *stabbed*. Even his mum's been to prison.'

'That's not a good thing.'

'Yeah, but he *knows* things. He's done stuff. Benjy's so worried about being *good* all the time. He's such a mummy's boy.'

Sam took a new packet of cigarettes out of his pocket. He peeled the cellophane off and screwed it into a ball.

'Where do you even get the money to smoke so much?'

'Punky's brother brings them over.'

'Punky's an idiot, Sam. You're horrible when you're with him. You were horrible to *me*. It was embarrassing.'

'You shouldn't have been out there. I told you, he's not right.'

'You don't know him.'

'Yeah, like you don't know Punky. He's not like everyone thinks. He cares about stuff. He sticks up for me.'

He lit a new cigarette, took a big drag.

'He does go too far though. I'm not saying he doesn't go too far.'

'Is that what happened with the tools, then? Punky went too far?'

'Don't be sarcastic.'

'I'm not! I just want to know.'

Sam looked at me, as if he was checking whether I meant it or not. He tapped his ash into the vodka lid.

'I don't know,' he said. 'It was messed up. We were drinking Supers in the alley – Punky'd got served at the corner shop – and your mate walked past. He had his shoulders right back, and that hard face he does, and he recognised me, obviously, seeing as he's living in my garden, but he acted like he didn't.

'He was wearing flip-flops and that red vest, God knows when he washes that thing, and Punky stepped out of his way, a big exaggerated step, as if he was show-ing him respect, and your mate just passed by without a blink.

'Leanne called something after him, I can't remem-ber what, she always does it, and then she asked Punky why he hadn't said owt. She started saying he'd been cheeked, and Punky got all wound up. He started going on about coming down here, and showing him what hard meant.'

Sam's eyes were sparkling now, as he sat cross-legged

166

in the middle of his bedroom floor. I didn't know how much it was to do with the vodka and how much it was to do with the story, but I curled my feet under myself. I just wanted to understand.

'That's how we met, you know. Me and Punk. I got in a fight on the rec with someone he hated, and he came up to me after and shook my hand, and offered me a fag. He thought I did that kind of thing all the time, and I just went along with it. It's like you just pretend and then it's true,' he said, and I remembered what it felt like to walk off the cricket pitch with Trick, those rockets exploding behind us.

'So, anyway, we waited for it to get dark, finished our Supers. I hated it, but I walked fastest. I stayed at the front. They kept going on about it being my yard and how I shouldn't stand for it and I just kept quiet and kept going.

'Dean couldn't believe the size of the gardens down our road, he thought we must be loaded, and Leanne was winding Punky up. I just ignored it all, thinking it'd be over in a minute, whatever was going to happen. The house was dark except for your room and I just wanted to go in and neck a pint of water and get into bed, but I couldn't. So I stood there drinking my beer, and waiting.

'Punky said Dad was a twat for leaving all his equipment down there, right next to them. He pretended to elbow the window at the back, and then Dean kicks the corrugated iron, hard as he can, and Punky just punches the window, knocks all the glass out with his elbow. He jumps in, and Dean follows him, and they're just crashing around in there.'

His eyes were wide and he was talking fast. One of his feet juddered, up and down, on the spot.

'Leanne couldn't believe it – she grabbed my T-shirt and wouldn't let go. Then they jumped out and started running, and we followed, and I really needed a drink of water because my mouth was so dry, but there was no way I could go home now.

'We ran right past our house, up the road, and no one even noticed. I didn't even think about Dad. Or Mum. It was like we were the only people in the world.'

He looked at me, out of breath from talking so much, and I was so involved that when Dad called up the stairs, I let out a little shout.

'Two minutes!' he said.

I held my throat. My pulse was throbbing there. Sam laughed at me, but I couldn't join in.

'Don't think much of me these days, do you, Eye?'

I looked at him, sitting cross-legged, holding his mug of water as though it might warm his hands. His brown eyes were sad though his dimple was out. There were red creases on his cheeks from where he'd been lying face down all day.

'I do,' I said finally. 'I just don't think this *is* you.'

He held his arms out, arrogantly. 'This is me, Eyeball, so you'd better get used to it.'

I shook my head. We stared at each other, and then his smile dropped.

'Shit! What'm I gonna say? When he asks why I did it? What shall I say?'

I shrugged. 'Tell him what happened.'

He breathed in, long and slow, through his nose. His eyes were flat and empty suddenly.

'I'm pissed,' he said, and he looked worried, then started laughing. 'I'm chabongered!'

He stood, spun round in a circle. 'Wheeeee!'

The kitchen door opened, and Dad shouted up the stairs. 'On the table!'

Sam stopped spinning. 'I'm dead. D-ea-d.'

'You're not. Just clean your teeth. And be quiet.'

Walking down the stairs, I looked over my shoulder to see how he was doing. He held on to the wooden banister with his left hand, and slid his right, palm open, across the walls. His mouth moved up and down slightly at the corners, into a smile and out again. He looked demented.

'*Teeth,*' I hissed, pointing to the bathroom. 'You stink.'

'I'm dead,' he giggled as he brushed his teeth. Minty foam dribbled from his mouth.

I made him splash cold water on his face, again and again until he was angry with me, and then I left him wiping his neck with a towel, and I went into the kitchen.

Twenty-three

Dad wriggled a knife around the lasagne edges, scraping the welded bits of cheese and tomato from the dish so we got to eat the best bits.

'How hungry are you?' he asked.

'Very,' I said, though I felt too nervous to eat. He placed a thick stack of steaming pasta on my plate.

'Sam okay?' he asked.

'Just coming,' I said, using my fork to put the lasagne back into a neat tower. I didn't look at him. 'He's in the bog.'

The radio was playing dance music to get people in the mood for Friday night, but the fast beat and horns were going right to my guts and making me feel scared. I got up and switched the station to local.

Dad sang along.

'*Oh how I want to break free . . .*' he sang. He saw me

looking and closed his eyes as if he was lost in the music, and I smiled because he was trying.

He put two more stacked-high plates on the table, and took the garlic bread out the oven.

'H-h-h-hot,' he said, dropping it on the table with his bare hands.

'Why don't you just use an oven glove?' I said, because it was our routine since he had set ours on fire by mistake – and then the door opened, and Sam walked in.

His eyes were red, but he looked sober enough. He wasn't giggling or smirking at least. The neck of his T-shirt was damp and his clothes were creased from where he'd been lying on them all day. He *stank* of aftershave.

'Eat it while it's hot,' Dad said, and his voice sounded weird and high-pitched. He sat down, and sliced at his food with his fork, eating it straight away even though it burned him. He pulled air into his mouth as he chewed.

I stabbed my pile all over with my knife so it would cool down. The pineapple was always scalding. Next to me, Sam cut a cross in the middle of his. He lifted the pasta flaps and blew.

Dad didn't read for once. He stared out the window at the blue tits and robins and the goldcrest that landed on the bird table. Occasionally, he looked at Sam.

My appetite was fine, though I could feel the nerves as I ate, and I wondered what it would take for me to actually go off my food. I put some garlic bread on Sam's plate, hoping it would soak up the vodka in his belly.

We ate without talking, and the radio chattered on, and it wasn't long until everyone was finished.

'So,' Dad said.

He chucked the nubs of the garlic bread to Fiasco, one by one. Her jaws snapping shut around them was like a countdown.

'We're going to have to talk about this one, boy.'

Sam didn't look up.

I piled our plates and climbed around my brother to get out from the table. I scraped the leftovers we'd saved for Fiasco into her bowl.

'*Punky*,' Dad said, as if he were talking about an only very recently identified species of tree. 'Tell me about him.'

I ran the taps, and frothed the water. If I made myself useful Dad might let me stay.

'Sam?'

It was getting dark outside, and it was just enough so that the window worked as a kind of spyglass. In it I saw my brother raise his eyebrows.

'What?'

'Well? Where does he live? Who's his mum and dad?'

'Doesn't really have any.'

'No?' Dad's tone was strange. I didn't recognise it.

'Lives with his brother.'

'Where?'

'West End.'

'And how old's this brother?'

'How do I know?' Sam's face screwed up. 'Older.'

'I can leave you to the coppers if you want, boy.'

Sam started talking in a machine gun monotone. 'His brother's older than him, twenty maybe. His dad died. He don't see his mum.'

'So? What happened then? With the shed.'

Sam looked at Dad for the first time, and his expression was earnest. 'It was Punky's idea.'

'Well, *obviously*.'

'I told him about the gypsies, and he wanted to see for himself.' Sam's eyes flicked over to me, and I rinsed the suds from a plate quietly as I could.

Dad rubbed his brow.

'We thought if—'

'*We?* I thought it was Punky's idea?'

'It was! I thought we were just messing about, but then Punky smashed the window and jumped through it and then we were legging it through the fields . . .'

He stopped himself, but it was too late. He'd sounded excited.

'Sounds like fun! And you just stood there, did you? Through all this? Just let him get on with it?'

Sam dropped his head back onto his shoulders.

'*Get* that look off your face,' Dad barked, and he swiped at Sam's chin with his fingers.

Sam sat up straight.

A minute passed while Dad tried to find out why Punky got chucked out of school, and if he had a criminal record, and what his brother did for a living, and Sam told him that he didn't know and he wasn't sure and he had no idea, and all the time I kept my hands busy in the sink, expecting every second to be told to clear off.

Dad rubbed his throat, mulling it over.

'Nope,' he said. 'I still don't get it. Where's Benjy in all this?'

Sam's mouth opened, but nothing came out. He pressed his lips together, and I wanted him to say what he'd said to me, that Punky had been there for him, that he went too far but he was a friend, that Benjy was a baby: anything true. I willed him to at least try to make Dad understand.

'And where were you when Punky just *jumped through the window*? Why in flaming hell didn't you stop him?'

Sam sat forward, mouth open like he was going to explain, then slumped against the wall instead.

'Sam!' Dad shouted, half getting up from his chair, but his shouting didn't have the same effect as before.

The vodka had taken hold. 'I'm not messing about! You've got to help me out here!'

'What?' Sam shouted back, and he used the dead, sullen voice he saved for Dad. 'What d'you want me to say? I fell out with Benjy! So what? Punky's a mate. I don't know why we broke into your stupid shed. We were just having a laugh.'

'A *laugh*?'

'Yeah, *a laugh.*'

Sam stared at some point beyond Dad's head.

'Is that it then?' Sam said. 'Can I *go* now?'

'No, you can't bleeding *go*, you haven't told me owt yet.'

Sam sank his head back into his shoulders.

'Tough these days, aren't you? Real little hard man. This Punky's got you whipped, hasn't he?'

Sam's lip curled, but he wouldn't make eye contact.

'*Throw this boot on the roof, Sam. Break into your dad's shed.* Never mind that I'm the bugger who has to pay for it.'

'The boot was nothing to do with Punky.'

'*Whatever you say, Punky.*'

'You sound stupid.'

'*I* sound stupid?' Dad was almost laughing now, and it was a nasty laugh.

I moved my hands through the hot water in the sink, looking at the way the bubbles caught on the wooden bracelet Mum had sent me, breathing in the smell of washing-up liquid.

176

'You've not got a flaming clue, have you?' Dad said. 'Not a clue. What you sound like. What you *look* like. When I see you at the shops, sitting on that bench like you do, *smoking* and *spitting* . . .'

Sam raised his eyebrows. 'What?' He shrugged. He did an open-mouthed grin. 'What do you think, Dad? Are you ashamed of me? Are you, Dad? Are you ashamed of me?'

Dad didn't answer, but his head nodded ever so slightly as he stared back at Sam. He was struggling to keep himself together.

'Ah, fuck you,' Sam muttered, and he started to leave the table.

Dad leaned into him, half getting up himself. '*What* did you say?' he said, very quietly.

'I said . . . Fuck. You!' Sam shouted, and his face was quite grey as he jumped up. The table legs screeched on the kitchen floor as he pushed it away from him.

Dad was out of his seat too, and I couldn't see properly because he was in the way, but he'd gotten hold of Sam, and Sam had shrunk down on the bench. Dad's fists were twisting at the neck of Sam's white T-shirt.

'You're a loser. No wonder she left you! You're a prick!' Sam said, trying to yank Dad's hands off. He swung at him wildly, but Dad had too firm a hold.

After a few seconds Sam stopped struggling. Dad let him go.

I wiped my eyes, but my hands were wet too. I'd dripped water all down the front of my T-shirt.

'Pack it in!' I said. I wanted them to remember I was here now. 'Please don't.'

'Not such a hard man yet,' Dad said calmly, stepping away. He wiped his hands on the back of his jeans.

Sam held his head at the kitchen table.

'Now get out of it. I don't want to look at you.'

Sam stood slowly. His neck was blotchy and his cheeks were red as he walked to the middle of the kitchen, right next to where Dad stood.

'Always me, isn't it? Always bloody me. Why don't you ask *her* what she's been up to? Why don't you have one of your *little chats* with her?'

I stared at Sam. I couldn't believe it.

Dad turned to me, out of breath slightly. He wiped his hands over his face.

'Iris?' he said.

'Go on. *Ask her.*'

My mind went blank.

'She's been hanging around with that gypo again. At night.'

Dad dragged his hands down, pulling at his skin so his face looked like a drooping waxy mask.

'Right romantic it looked. Real Romeo and Juliet stuff.'

'But it *wasn't* him that broke into the shed, I *told*

you . . .' I started, but Dad held his hand out for me to stop. He looked so tired that my mouth snapped shut by itself.

'Get to your room,' he said quietly.

I opened the door to go, but Sam hadn't finished.

'Oh yeah, *go to your room*. *Real* punishment. Why don't you grab *her* round the neck, see how she likes that?'

'What did I just say to you?' Dad shouted at me because I was standing in the doorway like an idiot. 'Out! I've had it. That's *it*! That's your *flaming* lot.'

Sam was demanding to know where his trainers were. I couldn't hear what Dad was saying because he'd slammed the door in front of me, and adrenalin was rushing past my ears.

I sat on my bed for what seemed like hours, listening to them. I watched the moon rising out my bedroom window. It was full finally. I wished Mum was here.

I heard someone scuffling around in the cupboard under the stairs. There was some stomping and then Sam's bedroom door slammed. The outside kitchen door slammed too, and I was relieved. Dad had finally given up, and gone to the Stag.

I looked out my bedroom window at the tall hedge-rows of the paddock, and I thought of Trick less than a hundred metres away.

I opened my window and climbed out.

Twenty-four

One good hit. That was all I had. Any more and they'd get suspicious. Trick's dad's car was missing, but his Uncle Johnny's was parked up. He could be inside. The first acorn missed the white caravan; the second scuffed an edge. I searched for more. The third hit; a good solid, echoing hit. I prayed that Trick was in, that the telly wasn't on too loud, that he'd notice. I stared at the caravan door, willing it to open. And then it did.

Trick looked in the direction of the alder straight away. He lifted his hand, and I remembered this was the exact spot where we'd first met, when he'd caught me spying.

He ran to meet me, and we went to the stepping stones. Before I'd said anything he gave me a hug. His hair was damp. I started explaining, but I couldn't get it out right. I got to the part where Sam had tried to punch Dad but it didn't make any sense.

'They've both gone mad,' I said finally.

'Slow down,' Trick said. He wiped my eyes with his vest. It was warm and smelled like him, and I breathed in, and started again. I told him everything, including the fact that Sam and Punky had stolen the tools, and he didn't look surprised at all about that.

I told him that Dad knew we'd been seeing each other, that Sam had told him, that I'd never seen either of them so mad, and he told me that families fell out all the time, it didn't mean anything, that things would be better in the morning. We sat on the bank of the brook, and the sound of it trickling by was so peaceful that I began to calm down.

That's when we heard something. It was distant at first, but it got closer.

It chewed up the night around us. We ran across the stepping stones and through the pig farmer's field to get a better look.

In the shadows of the willows and alders by the ditch, we watched a tractor approach the paddock. Its lights hit the hedgerow, sent birds flying into the sky.

Dad walked into the field first with Fraz. The tractor lights turned them to silhouettes. The pig farmer was at the wheel. Behind came Billy Whizz, the rabbit catcher who brought us skinned rabbits and shot-filled pheasants, Big Chapmun, who worked on the Ashbourne Estate, and a few other men I recognised from The Stag or fishing trips or barbecues long ago. Even Austin was there, looking uncertain at the back. They all wore work boots and gloves.

Trick swore, and sprinted to his mum and dad's caravan. In the doorway, Nan stood wide-eyed in a dressing gown. I felt sorry for her. I didn't care that she'd lied about needing water, or that she was on our land.

I pressed myself against the wood, wishing I was a stick insect; that I could disappear against trees and leaves, that nothing made a difference to me.

Trick jumped down from the caravan steps. His hair shone gold in the headlights, and he held his hand out to shield his eyes. Dad's face was grim. The pig farmer let the engine idle.

'Me da isn't in! It's just me mammy and me sisters! We'll move ourselves. Let me just go and get me da.'

I heard Dad shout something, but couldn't hear what. It was clear from his face that he was past caring. Dad waved at the pig farmer, and the tractor revved again.

Trick ran past them, headed out of the paddock. I ran through the pig farmer's field fast as I could to try and intercept him. He was halfway to the top of the road when a motorbike came powering in. Its pale yellow light bounced across the road, picking out lumps of brick and stones, making the potholes look deeper than they were. It charged at Trick, and he jumped into the trees at the side of the road. It carried on towards me, its lights making me squint, and in a storm of whoops and revs Sam and Punky passed by.

Punky turned the motorbike around, tyres screeching, and it roared past me again, stopping in a diagonal, across Trick's path.

Sam jumped off the back. He was wearing his football boots and no helmet. Punky walked the motorbike over to block Trick in, but Trick wouldn't give up. He tried to use the grassy verge to get round them.

Sam put his hand on his chest.

'Get your hands off me,' Trick said.

'Hey, hey, *hey*,' Punky said. I'd caught up with them now, and I saw his horrible slow smile as he talked to Trick.

Trick told them to get out of his way; that he had to get somewhere.

'What's the rush?' Sam asked. His lips were wet and he was smiling stupidly.

I told him to leave Trick alone, but I was worried about Trick going to get his dad too. I kept picturing his face when he found out what was happening in the paddock, the way he would knock back his pint and rush to the car. Him and Johnny would tear back to the caravans, and then what?

'Sam, leave him,' I shouted, but it was too late, they were chesting up to each other. Punky laughed as I tried to get between them. 'Stop it!' I said.

There was a shout from the top of the road.

'Baby!'

Leanne walked onto the lane with Dean and her pit bull.

She had a two-litre bottle of cider with the label peeled off, and her cap was propped up on her forehead, peak pointed to the sky. When she saw what was happening she laughed, and started running. Dean trailed behind, as uninterested as ever. The pit bull raced ahead, stopping at Punky's heels to bark and snap at him.

'Pikelet!' she cheered, and her tone was so light it made me shudder. '*Hello there!*'

Her Irish accent was Scottish.

'Come *on*,' Trick shouted. 'Get out my friggin' way.' His voice was desperate as he tried to get away, and you could just hear the tractor in the distance, and then there was a smack as Sam thumped him in the chin.

'Trick!' I shouted.

Trick moved back, shifting his feet into a better stance, and I remembered Matt Dunbar's head cracking on the tarmac.

Punky shouted encouragement to Sam as the two boys weighed each other up. The pit bull circled them,

184

yelping. Leanne watched, excited, her big mouth hanging open. Dean lit a new cigarette.

Sam ran at Trick. He grabbed him round the waist, trying to push him over while Trick dug his fist into Sam's ribs. Sam stepped away, winded. He held one palm out to keep Trick back. I rushed in, putting a hand on Sam's shoulder and Trick's chest, begging them not to fight. I pushed like the hero when the walls are closing in, but with less success.

Leanne's dog growled at my heels as I pleaded with each of them to leave it, and then Punky grabbed me, and walked me back to the side of the road. He twisted my arm behind my back and pushed it upwards.

'Stay out of it, girlie,' he whispered, and his breath was hot against my ear. It smelled like he was getting a cold.

Trick's expression was stuck somewhere between disgust and pity. He started to walk off as Sam hunched over, panting.

'I told you already. You're not going *anywhere*,' Sam shouted, and he launched himself after Trick, but he'd left himself open, and Trick turned round and cracked him straight in the face. There was an awful popping noise and Trick's knuckles came away slippery and wet with blood.

'Prick!' Punky shouted.

Sam ran his fingers over his nostrils, flicking blood from his fingertips. Trick brushed his knuckles on the sides of his white vest, smearing red around his middle. He guarded his face with his fists.

'Nothing I hate more than an unfair fight,' Punky said.

'He's had training all right,' Dean said.

'Sly not to mention it,' Leanne said, and I hated her most out of them all.

The two boys closed in.

They stood on either side of Sam, and I thought of Punky's Stanley knife, the blade yoiked up, and I tried again to get between them. Leanne grabbed hold of me. I could hear her giggle as she held my arms, my personal straitjacket. She was so strong but her laugh was so childish. It was horrible.

I didn't know if I wanted to get to Sam or Trick now Sam was hurt, I just wanted to stop things, but whenever I moved, Leanne was there. She let go of my arms after a while, and stood in front of me, blocking my way like the most aggressive marker in the history of netball.

She was enormous and fast, and I only saw bits.

Trick smashed Punky's chin and swung Sam out the way. Dean ran at Trick's waist, barging it with his shoulder like an American football player. Punky and Dean got hold of Trick's arms while Sam stamped against his chest. The metal studs on his football boots flashed in the moonlight.

Struggling to get round Leanne, I fell over. When I

got up, she hit me. Her silver sovereign slammed against my temple. I held my head for a second. When I looked again, Sam was stepping away, winded. I wondered vaguely if he had his inhaler. He bent over to get his breath back, and I was so relieved he was out of the fight I shouted encouragement to Trick.

He was the best fighter by miles, but Dean and Punky worked together. I could hardly watch.

Punky kicked him in the back, while Dean headbutted him, holding on to his ears. Trick's face was swollen on one side, and blood was trickling from a nasty-looking gash on the side of his head. I couldn't believe he was still standing. He doubled over, and I thought this time he was really going down, but he only crouched on the floor for a second to get his balance.

He watched the two of them with big, white-filled eyes, one hand protecting his face, the other scratching at the floor. His expression reminded me of something, I couldn't remember what, and then I saw his fist curl around a chunk of brick.

As Sam charged in, Trick reared up. Heaving Dean from his shoulders, he brought down the hand holding the brick, and there was a loud crack, and Sam fell.

I ran to see if he was all right. Leanne had stopped marking me. We were on the same side suddenly. She knelt by Sam's head, shouting his name, but he was unconscious.

Punky and Dean held their hands out, like footballers denying a foul. Trick cupped his ear, which was covered in blood. He stared at us, fierce-eyed and white-faced, still bobbing slightly. Blood was caught in the dips between his fingers. The front of his vest was freckled with it. Red hand marks smeared around his waist.

'You've killed him,' Punky said, and he moved towards Sam as if he was going to shake him. I told him to get away.

'You can't move them,' Leanne said.

'What have you done?' I kept saying to Trick, and then Leanne shouted at me to calm the hell down, and I realised I was screaming.

Time was sticky and thick as I sat beside Sam. He'd fallen sideways, and one arm was folded next to him, the other stretched out as if he'd been reaching for something. His eyes were closed, and blood was making its way from the wound near his temple to the ground. It ran across his eye, and down his nose, a thin red stream.

I couldn't stop saying his name.

Punky had backed off to where he'd dropped the motorbike.

'Ride to a phone box and call an ambulance, and I'll wait here,' I said, but he wasn't listening.

Leanne pulled at his arm. '*James*, we've got to ride to the phone box.'

Punky ignored her. He spoke to Dean. 'I'll take Lee home, and get rid of the bike. You just get out of here.'

Dean nodded, then turned and sprinted off. I shouted after him to call an ambulance.

Leanne was crying now, black tears full of eyeliner, and it seemed impossible that I could have been scared of her less than a minute ago.

Punky kick-started the motorbike.

'Get on,' he shouted. 'Hurry up.'

She opened her mouth as if to say something, but Punky thrashed the accelerator again, and she clambered on, clinging to his back like a baby monkey.

The pit bull chased after them.

My blood was shifting back to something more normal. It was like waking up. I checked Sam's pulse, asked him questions. I could feel his heartbeat, strong and violent.

'Go and phone an ambulance,' Trick said, and his voice was flat and insistent and I realised he'd been saying the same thing for a long time. 'I'll wait here. You go and phone an ambulance.'

I was leaving when Sam started to shake. He lay on his back, limbs and torso thrashing madly. I couldn't remember what to do. I checked there was nothing hard under his head, but the whole ground was covered in stones.

Pink foam pooled at the corner of his mouth, blood and spit mixed. It spurted out of him, and I wiped it away with the corner of my T-shirt. I asked him to please wake up, and told him he was going to be all right, and all the time blood trickled from the side of his head.

I told Trick not to dare leave my brother, and I went to get help.

Twenty-five

My teeth were chattering and my lungs about to burst when I got to the paddock. Trick's uncle's trailer had been moved to block the entrance. Nan's face dropped when she saw me. She stood in the doorway of her caravan, wrapped in a long wool cardigan now. The tractor was so loud. The little black dog yapped at her ankles, but I couldn't hear it. I could see the feet of one of Trick's little sisters poking out behind her. The greyhounds barked at the tractor tyres, scratching at the ground underneath them.

Once you were in the glare of the tractor's lights, the rest of the field disappeared. Dad was bent in front of one the caravans. Its tow bar had been looped with chains and stacked with timber, and Dad was grunting with the effort of shifting it. The tea towel he'd wrapped around his knuckles was covered in black grease.

'What?' he shouted over the noise of the tractor

engine, and he sounded annoyed until he saw my expression.

'Where's Sam?' he said.

'There's been an accident,' I said, and the words vibrated through my teeth. 'I've rung for an ambulance.'

He waved his arms at the pig farmer, shouted to turn the bloody engine off. The tractor coughed to silence. The lights cut. The field stank of exhaust fumes.

'There's been a fight,' I stuttered. 'Sam's hurt. He's at the top of the road. The ambulance is coming.'

In the moonlight, Dad's skin was grey. He put his hands on my shoulders, looking as if he was about to ask another question, then he grabbed a torch from Fraz, and took off. I followed, stumbling over the tufts of long grass. A bird flew up from somewhere near my feet.

I thought I would fall, but my legs kept moving and my lungs kept filling up. The moon floated above me.

I was crying now, and shivering. I couldn't stop. Sam was dead. I knew it. He'd lost so much blood.

I chased Dad up the lane. His torchbeam caught the tyre marks that scarred the dirt track, and I looked at them, hoping somehow Sam wouldn't be there, that he'd be sitting at the side of the road, that he'd only been unconscious, but he was exactly where I'd left him.

Trick had gone. I was so angry. Then something caught my eye. He was in the pig farmer's field, a few metres off. He crouched behind a patch of nettles, on the other side of the hedge, and his face showed no sign that he'd seen me, though his eyes were on mine.

It was like we were seeing each other for the first or last time. Something went through me, and then he turned and ran, towards the stepping stones and the paddock.

In the torchlight, I saw Sam's face. His nostrils were crusted with blood, and his nose was a mess, flat where it shouldn't be. Blood had turned the hair around the cut on his head black and thick and glossy, and there was a shiny pool of it beneath him.

'My God,' Dad said.

He held his ear over Sam's mouth, listening for breath. He checked his pulse.

'Sam,' I said. 'Wake up. Sammy? Can you hear me?'

His hand was warm against mine. 'Is he there?' I kept saying, instead of is *it* there, meaning his pulse, but I couldn't hear Dad's answer because my teeth were chattering so much. The night was balmy, but I was freezing cold.

Dad found the cleanest part of his tea towel and pressed it to Sam's temple. He told me to hold it there, to keep the pressure on, and I was scared in case I made it worse, but he shouted until I pressed as hard as he wanted. He took his jumper off and lay it across Sam's chest.

'Sam,' Dad called sharply. 'Can you hear me? Sam? Say something. God, I'm so sorry, Sam. You're all right though, you're all right, boy. You're going to be all right.'

Sam groaned. His eyes opened.

'Dad?'

'I'm so sorry, Sam. I'm so sorry.'

'What for?'

Putting his thumb in his mouth, he hooked his broken nose with his finger. He felt for his chicken pock scar then winced. 'I've got toothache.'

'Yeah, we're going to get that sorted,' Dad said. 'We're going to the dentist now. Are you warm enough?'

Sam rolled over and spat a mouthful of blood. His brown eyes settled on mine. I couldn't think. I stroked his stubbly head.

'Hiya, Sam,' I said, stupidly, and then he lay back and his eyes closed again.

'That's it, nice and warm now,' Dad said, tucking his jumper under Sam's chin.

He rubbed one hand over his chest.

'Nice and warm,' he said.

He took my hand and squeezed it, and we sat like that, the three of us, me and Dad watching the lights of the cars on Ashbourne Road swing by, hoping that the next ones would be blue, that they would slow down and turn towards us.

Twenty-six

I sat in the waiting room of Intensive Care with my head throbbing. I felt like I was sitting in a foggy room. When I turned my head I saw stars. We'd watched the paramedics bring Sam in on a stretcher. They'd put IVs in his arms, and given him a tetanus jab, and rushed him to have a CT scan.

He was almost the same colour as his pillow, and just as still, and Dad had clutched my shoulders as they wheeled him to where he needed to be. I'd been checked over and except for a lump and bit of bruising, I was fine; a mild concussion.

Dad sat beside me, and I realised my hand was boiling hot because he was holding it. He rubbed it between his palms, and I felt his chapped skin.

He half shouted my name, and I opened my eyes, frightened.

'You can't sleep, Eye. Remember,' he said, gently.

He held out a plastic cup of tea, and I wondered where it had come from. Strip lights blinded me. There was a fuzzy feeling in my head, like my brain had been swapped for a huge bumblebee. I narrowed my eyes as it shifted position.

A pale nurse with long dark hair and red lips walked out from Sam's ward. Dad told me to wait while he tried to talk to her.

I sipped the too sweet tea.

He caught up with her at another doorway. He looked really old next to the young nurse.

She shook her head, and her dark ponytail brushed against her back. Dad rubbed his face. She shook her head again and touched his arm, and Dad nodded slowly, and then she went away.

'Nothing new. A doctor will come and talk to us soon,' he said.

He sat back down.

Sam had been sedated to stop the seizures. They'd gotten worse after we arrived.

Dad asked again what the hell had happened out there. From the start, he said. He took my shoulders, and looked into my eyes.

'Who was out there, Iris? Was it that gypsy? Was Punky there?'

I couldn't answer. I thought of Trick's fingers scrabbling on the ground, the wet sound of Sam's nose breaking. I opened my mouth. Dad had oil on his cheek.

'Iris. Your brother could . . . Sam could . . .' His voice buckled before he finished the sentence, and he looked away, down the never-ending tunnel of the hospital corridor.

I wiped my eyes. 'I know,' I said. '*I know*. But I *don't know*.' And it sounded so mournful it could have been true.

He held me away from him, and checked my expression.

'You don't remember?'

He examined the lump on my head.

'Because that isn't good.'

He began looking around for a nurse, but there were only more people like us – confused and scared, or worn down and used to it, flicking blindly through magazines. He pressed the side of my head and I winced.

'Sam'll be okay,' he said. 'And your memory will come back. It's just the concussion. You'll be all right.'

He let go of my hand and stood, looking up and down the corridors for a nurse. He rubbed his hand over his chin, and sat down again.

'Us Dancys are tough,' he said. 'Specially our noggins.'

He tried to smile. There were stars behind my eyes. They floated around the edges of things. The walls of the waiting room were a dull blue.

I heard the noise of them scratching and grunting and scraping. I heard Leanne's high-pitched laugh. I saw Sam's head in a pool of blood. I wanted to sleep.

Dad put his arm round me.

'No sleep. Come on. Talk to me.'

He rubbed my arm too hard, and I opened my eyes.

'The police will need to talk to you. Soon as your brother wakes up. You'll have to give a statement. Tell them who did it.'

I nodded, squeezing my eyes shut against his chest. I wanted to tell him everything, but I couldn't speak.

The doctor arrived. She introduced herself as Dr Kang, and gave us a quick, kind smile. She took the plastic seat beside Dad. Her perfume was sweet, and there was a big ink spot on the pocket of her white shirt. She started talking straight away.

'Your son's stable for the moment. We've put him on anti-convulsant medications to control the seizures. I'm afraid the CT scan showed a skull fracture, and swelling as well as bleeding in the brain. Your son needs emergency surgery. We're preparing to take him to the operating theatre.'

She explained how surgeons would cut a small hole in Sam's skull and insert a plastic tube to drain some of the fluid from inside the brain and help relieve the pressure. They would take out the blood clots too. We nodded, as if we could understand. I kept thinking about *how* they would cut a small hole in Sam's skull.

As Dr Kang was getting up to go, Dad told her that my concussion was worse than we'd thought, that I didn't remember anything about what had happened at all. I thought I'd see suspicion in her brown eyes, but she only said I would be fine, as long as he watched the symptoms carefully and saw a doctor if they got any worse. She said the best thing he could do for me was take me home to get some rest.

'We'd rather wait here,' Dad said, and the doctor talked about the possibility of a family room, but Dad said we were fine where we were. She gave a pointed look to me, but I agreed with him.

'We won't be comfortable anywhere,' I said.

Before she left, she told Dad not to rush me.

'These things can be very traumatic for young witnesses,' she said, and I wanted to hug her, until the words sank in.

I was now a witness.

Twenty-seven

We were allowed to see Sam for a few minutes during the night. He had a tube coming out of bandages on his head. Something about keeping the pressure in his brain under control. It looked scary. He was still pale, and more tubes came out of his mouth and nose, and he had little suckered wires stuck to his chest as well as IVs in each arm.

The room was cold, because the doctors were lowering Sam's temperature to try and decrease the swelling in his skull. He'd been put on a ventilator. The sucking, wheezing sounds made me think of my lungs inside me.

Dad held Sam's hand and told him he was proud of him, that he loved him, that he was sorry.

'When you wake up, I'll make it up to you,' he said, really quietly, and he looked half embarrassed as he spoke.

I stood at the foot of the bed, unable to think anything except: *You're my brother, you're my brother, you're my brother*.

Twenty-eight

I woke curled across two seats with my head on the jumper Dad had used to cover Sam. It smelled of metal, and when I lifted it, I saw blood. I felt sick.

'What time is it?' I asked, but Dad didn't answer. He was looking out the window. We were high up, on the fifth floor. I could see fields out the window, and a white water tower.

'You wouldn't hold back, would you? You'd just tell the truth, wouldn't you?'

He turned to study me, and I nodded, but my throat was closing, and I wondered if I'd ever be able to talk to him again.

'Things I said to him, Iris. Why would I say those things?'

He looked so confused.

The sun was beginning to filter through the blinds that covered the windows, and he pulled at the cord, but it didn't do anything. He let go, and it rattled for a few seconds.

'All that blood,' he choked, and I felt myself drowning in it too.

Twenty-nine

At eight o'clock, Dr Kang came to talk to us. She had a clean shirt on and the same sweet perfume. She asked how my head was, then started talking in her rapid way.

'The plan now is to see if we can bring your son out of his coma. We'll turn the lorazepam off and see if he's seizure free. If we can successfully bring him off the lorazepam, that will tell us a lot. Off the meds we'll be able to see how well his brain is functioning, for better or worse.'

We had questions as always, but she couldn't give us any answers.

'It sounds basic, but I'm afraid it's true. All we can do at this point is wait and see. We won't know the extent of the damage until we can bring him out of the coma. Until then, we do everything we can to make him comfortable.'

I'd read the pamphlets they'd left. Brain damage could result in paralysis, amnesia, loss of vision, loss of intellect, loss of speech, changes in personality. Dad said he didn't care, as long as Sam woke up, but what if he woke up dribbling and dense and needing a nappy?

We got a taxi home to change our clothes, and clean our teeth and collect things for Sam. At the top of our road Dad asked the taxi driver to stop. He wanted to walk.

The sky was bright blue and white, and the firs choked with birdsong. In a garden nearby somebody yodelled as they watered the plants.

Trees hadn't uprooted and stones hadn't split. Birds hadn't fallen from the sky, didn't lie rotting on the ground, but a few metres from where Sam had fallen we found the motorbike. Its scorched black frame leaned in a pool of melted rubber and metal, and I imagined Punky and Leanne and Dean coming back to leave it here in the early hours of the morning, dropping a match into the petrol tank in Sam's honour, and running as fast as they could, listening out for the explosion.

The bottom half of each tyre had turned to charcoal and ash, but the tops were untouched, and the track there was still perfect. Dad lifted a teardrop of liquefied metal from the ruins, and held it out to me like a jewel.

'This jog your memory?'

He wouldn't stop looking at me, and I couldn't tell when would be a normal time to stop shaking my head.

He put the jewel in his pocket, and we trudged back to the house.

Big Chapmun's tractor sat on the drive. It was caked in mud, but it gleamed in the sun. I remembered Trick's hair glowing in its lights a thousand years ago when he'd shouted at them to stop, but just as quickly he was gone.

Thirty

I was cleaning my teeth when Dad shouted.

'Iris? Come up here a minute.'

He was standing by the window in his bedroom. I knew what I'd see before I saw it.

The paddock was empty.

The hollow feeling in my gut expanded. It pressed against my throat.

The fire had been kicked out, and there was a scalded black patch left. Charred logs were strewn in the long grass nearby. Two yellow rectangles marked where the caravans had been. Rubbish had spread further around the paddock: nappies and the insides of toilet rolls and empty food cartons and scrunches of tin foil. The pile of scrap. The washing line that had been attached to one of the caravans drooped to the ground, still attached to an alder.

Dad sat on his bed. The mattress wheezed as he

shifted position. I didn't ever want to stop looking out the window.

The sky was cartoon-bright, big white clouds against the blue, and across the brook, the maize flowers of the cornfield waved in the breeze.

I could feel Dad looking at me, working it out, and I dropped onto the bed beside him. The silence between us grew into a gigantic, living thing. It pressed against my neck and forced me to start talking.

I told him the truth, all of it – that I'd gone to see Trick after the argument, that I was hiding by the ditch when he'd arrived in the tractor, that Sam had started it – and my voice sounded small and far away, like it was coming from a radio somewhere high above us.

When I got to the bit where it was Sam, Punky and Dean against Trick, Dad raised a finger. He put it very close to my face.

'Don't you dare defend him,' he said, and he spoke very quietly and slowly. The muscles in his face were working like mad. 'I don't *ever* want to hear you defend that *thug* again.'

I felt the corn den and Trick, and this whole summer, the way it had been, slipping away from me, becoming something else.

After a million years, he looked at me again, and his eyes were cold.

'You know, not very long ago, I wouldn't have believed you *could* lie to me. Not very long ago at all.'

Outside the window the poplars shimmied in the breeze, and I noticed how if you really looked, each leaf had its own little dance. They never stopped moving, just did their dance up there, over and over, and for nobody.

Thirty-one

A cobweb heavy with dust hung from my bedroom ceiling. I noticed how even when you couldn't cry any more, your body hurt with wanting to. Trick was gone. Dad had been right. Sam might die. The insides of my veins ached, and my fingertips throbbed. Fiasco squirmed beside me, trying to lick my face.

Dad was in the shower now. Water slapped the bath as he washed. The sun shone through my curtains, and I watched the shadow of the rose bush dance across the wall.

I had drifted into a kind of trance when I realised the shadow had swollen, that there was a scratching noise at the glass.

Fiasco jumped off the bed, and ran to the window. She let out a high-pitched bark. I opened the curtains.

My heart plummeted or leaped. I couldn't tell, but it made me dizzy.

Trick stood behind the rose bush.

Dad would kill me. He would kill him. I couldn't talk to him. *But he'd waited*. He hadn't run away.

He wore the same clothes as last night, and his face was bruised and swollen on one side, with his bottom lip split, and I thought how he'd been right weeks ago about his nose ending up broken again before long because there was a flat bit at the top where his black eyes started that was the exact shape of a flint arrowhead.

I opened the window.

Trick pressed his lips together. Underneath the freckles on his nose the skin was turning lilac. His tanned face was pale, but he looked calm.

He held his hands out to me, but I didn't take them.

'My dad's in the shower,' I whispered. I could hear the water running. Any minute now it would stop.

Trick nodded.

'I couldn't go with them,' he whispered. 'They all went, but I kept seeing you, the way you looked at me, when your da came out, when I . . . Will you come out here, Iris? Please?'

I was a metre away from him. Only my desk and the window and the walls of the house were between us. He held his hands out to me but I couldn't look at them. My face had frozen. It had forgotten how to express itself. He put his hands in his back pockets, took them out again. He rested one against the wall.

211

'How is he?' he said, and he swallowed the last word.

I looked at the windowsill. There were paw prints and mud flakes and burrs from where the cats climbed in and out. I brushed the bits into a pile.

'Not good.' My voice was robotic and flat, and I got that feeling again, that I was listening to myself on a radio. It was hard to get the words out. My throat hurt. 'They think he might have brain damage. But they can't tell till he wakes up. They've put him in a coma because his brain's swelling inside his skull. He had to have emergency surgery.'

It was strange to say, and the way Trick looked it must have been strange to hear too.

'Thought he was dead,' he said.

He took some of the windowsill debris between his thumb and finger and scattered it on the grass.

'I'm so relieved,' he said, but he didn't sound relieved.

'Come out here,' he said, and it was a plea, plain and simple, but I couldn't move. He pushed his hair back off his face with his hand and took a big breath in and out, and all the time he looked at me. His face was so pale.

'Me mammy panicked when I told her, started packing up. I kept telling her to stop, to sit down and listen, but she wouldn't. She said we had to go, that she knew something like this would happen, that we could take me to hospital on the way. She wouldn't shut up, she'd lost it.'

He went to pull at his lip, but stopped in time.

'She woke the little ones soon as me da got back from the pub. He was so late. They had a screaming row, and I couldn't take it. Had to get out. I said I'd grab the things from outside, and I could hear them, me da swearing about what an unbelievable eejit I was, and how it wasn't his fault, he'd warned me, and I just stood out there.

'I couldn't leave . . . I couldn't let you think . . . It was bad enough that . . . Without . . . I just ran through the brook – I didn't even use the stepping stones – I ran straight through, and I ended up in the corn den.

'I could hear them from there, Iris, shouting their heads off: me da saying what would happen if I didn't come out, me mammy saying she wouldn't leave without me, Uncle Johnny trying to calm them down. She refused to go, and the girls were just wailing. They didn't know what was going on. I climbed the oak tree, and sat there, watching them till he won, and she gave up, like she always does.

'I didn't think they would really go. I don't know what I thought. But they got in the car and pulled away, and I was so relieved. I kept thinking your da was going to come back. I didn't want any more . . .

'Me mammy left an address,' he said, and I imagined her, half mad with worry, her hands at her red hair. 'Some cousins in Nottingham.'

'You can have it,' he said, meaningfully. 'In case . . . So you can let me know. What happens.'

His hand shook as he held out the scrap of paper, and I realised he wasn't calm at all.

'Surprised you can bear to look at me to be honest,' he said, and he almost pulled at his swollen top lip again.

I didn't know what to say. My head was empty as a balloon.

'I didn't know what was happening, Iris. They were all coming for me. I didn't know it was your brother. I swear. I just wanted them off me. I was waiting to be knifed. It wasn't the first time either, you know. I didn't tell you because the way you talk about him, I didn't want you to think . . . I'd've fought them weeks ago, but every time they started, on the road, or in the village, I just took it. I let it wash over me, because . . .'

He looked at me like he was considering something, and his face was tense as he lifted up his vest. His stomach was a mess of scabs and gashes. I remembered Punky and Dean holding his arms, Sam's football studs catching the moonlight.

'I was defending myself, Iris. I didn't want any of it. You know I didn't. I was trying to get to me da, that's all. I told you it comes for me, didn't I? You saw, didn't you? You saw.'

I examined his blond-tipped eyelashes, and the

crooked nose and the freckles there. He wanted so much for me to say it was true, but I couldn't do it.

'You hit my brother, over the head, with a brick.'

Trick looked at the ground. He crossed one arm over his belly, like he was holding himself together. He nodded his head, very slow.

'I'm sorry,' he said, and his voice was different now, flat.

There was the longest pause while I looked at the way his pupil leaked into his grey iris, and I couldn't speak, and then a pigeon beat out of a poplar nearby, and I realised the water had stopped running in the bathroom.

The pull-string of the electric shower twanged. Trick heard it too. He opened his arms out one last time.

'Please, Iris,' he said, so quietly I almost missed it.

I was so confused because Sam was in hospital, and Dad couldn't look at me, but more than anything I needed a hug, and so I climbed onto my desk and jumped into the front garden.

The sun was warm on my face, and I could smell the roses on the bush and feel their thorns against my back. I breathed in the sweat and smokiness of him. I tried to ignore the cold smell of metal underneath.

I looked up at him, and he stroked my cheek, and whatever my brain thought, the butterflies in my ribcage batted away.

He looked down at me, very directly, and his eyes were uncertain as always, but his voice was not uncertain at all.

'I never wanted any of it,' he said, and then he pulled away from me really quick.

He coughed, a big, spluttering cough, into a tissue he pulled from his pocket. It was ragged and wet with blood.

'I'm all right,' he said, wiping his mouth, and stuffing the tissue back in his pocket.

'Trick, you've got to go to hospital.'

'I will.'

I realised that the whole time he'd been standing here, he'd kept one hand on the wall, had been leaning slightly, and I wondered if he could actually take his own weight. For the first time I wondered how he was going to get to Nottingham.

'It's not just a broken nose this time, Trick.'

'I know.'

The lock on the bathroom door scraped open then, and without thinking about it, I was scrambling into my bedroom.

When I turned back, Trick had gone.

Thirty-two

Monday night, at seven o'clock, Dad waited by the phone. He picked it up before the first ring had finished, and told Mum what had happened. His voice was cold, right until the end.

'Sh-sh-sh,' he said to her then. 'You know what his head's made of. He'll be okay.'

The way he nudged the phone at my arm, I could tell he thought hearing me might help.

Tess picked her up from the airport, and brought her to the hospital early the next morning. Benjy trailed behind, carrying Mum's rucksack. I hadn't seen him for ages. His hair had grown long, almost to his shoulders. He'd started wearing black band T-shirts and long shorts instead of sports clothes, but he looked as shy and awkward as ever – the same old Benjy.

Mum walked into the waiting room, where we were

sitting together, pretending to read books we'd brought.

'How is he?' she said, breathless, her eyes frightened.

Dad told her the latest, that we were waiting to see if he could be brought out of his coma. His voice was hollow, and when he'd finished talking he told me he was going to get a cup of tea from the vending machine, and it was like she hadn't come in at all.

She'd cut all her hair off and it had turned white blond in the sun, and she was skinnier than before, wearing these weird baggy beige trousers. Her thin white shirt was creased all over, and her left wrist was full of wooden bracelets like the one she'd sent me. Her freckles had joined together and taken over her face, and all of these things, except the creases in her shirt, made her look out of place in the hospital.

She walked towards me, arms held open, and I just froze, until she was right there. I let her wrap me up.

She rubbed her hands over my shoulders roughly in a way I'd forgotten about and clasped the back of my head so it felt small and precious, and I could feel the rings on her fingers digging in and the hardness of her nails and all of it felt so familiar and smelled just the same as ever except perhaps more like coconut, and when she looked at me and said my name, that, out of all the things that had happened, made me cry the most.

Tess had brought cheese sandwiches and apples and grapes, and Mum had football magazines for when Sam woke up and nobody felt like telling her he'd been kicked off the team since she left. Benjy held a box of chocolates which, after a couple of hours, we opened for ourselves because we were so restless and, as Mum pointed out, they sold them in the shop just along the corridor so it wasn't like we couldn't get any more.

We shared them around with everybody, the hazelnut and caramels going first, just like they did on Christmas Day, and between the two of them, Mum and Tess managed to make the atmosphere a bit more like a really depressing coffee morning than the waiting room of Intensive Care.

Mum kept repeating the positives: Sam hadn't broken his neck, or damaged his spine. She asked me over and over about the moment he'd woken up.

'Definitely a good sign,' Tess said when I told her that he'd looked frightened, and Mum agreed, though she looked as if she might lie down on the floor and die herself.

Dad was gone for ages longer than it took to drink a cup of tea, and when he came back Mum went, mumbling about replacing the chocolates and checking there was time left on the car.

Benjy ran after her, and I saw her smile gratefully at him before they disappeared down the corridor.

I moved over so Dad could sit next to me, but he took a seat on the opposite row.

In his hand was the jewel from the burned-out motorbike.

Tess went to sit by him. She told him he looked well, which was a bit of a lie, and that she was happy to see him, which clearly wasn't a lie at all, and then she went over the positives again, very softly.

Dad looked at her, and I thought he was going to ask her to stop with the nonsense, but instead he started talking.

'I almost had it sorted. I was right in the middle of it, finally getting rid, and then . . . I almost had it sorted, Tess.'

I kept my eyes down, scared he was going to move on to how I'd disappointed him, how all summer I'd lied, but he just rubbed at his teardrop of metal. He rubbed and rubbed at it, and it made him look so mad I wished somebody would take it off him.

Tess put her hand over his, the empty one, and squeezed.

'Tough summer, eh, Tommo?'

Dad pressed his lips together. He let out a shaky breath, and shook his head.

Mum and Dad took turns to sit in the waiting room. Mum was self-conscious when Dad was around, and Dad acted all gruff and surly, so it was a relief when one or other of them cleared out. I started to dread the doctors coming. They never had any good news.

The CT scans continued to show swelling on Sam's brain. If things got worse the surgeons would have to operate again, and that had its own risks.

Dad told Tess his version of what had happened, and Tess told Mum. I couldn't talk about it. Whenever Dad started up about finding the gypsy who'd done this to his boy, and making him take responsibility, I felt like he was daring me to contradict him, right there in the waiting room of Intensive Care. I spent a lot of time in the toilet cubicle staring at my feet.

I thought of Trick, the way he'd turned away from me, to spit blood into his tissue, and I hoped he'd made it to Nottingham, or to hospital. I felt guilty for not trying to help him more. I felt guilty for worrying about him. I stared at my feet.

We'd eaten another grim canteen lunch and I was getting teas for Dad and Tess and coffee for Mum when I saw the sign for Accident and Emergency. It was on the floor below, and I was out of breath when I reached the desk. I asked if a Patrick Delaney had admitted himself. The man on the desk asked if I was a relative and I nodded. I was his sister.

He looked at me, typing, and reading his computer screen.

'No Delaneys,' he said.

I spelled it out for him, just in case, and he shook his head. 'Sorry. No.'

'He's got blond hair, gingerish maybe? A bit older than me. He had cuts and bruises all over his stomach. He'd been coughing up blood.'

The man's expression changed. 'Was an ambulance called?'

My guts twisted. It hadn't even crossed my mind.

The man behind the desk was looking at me suspiciously now.

'Where are your parents?' he said, scanning the room behind me. 'How old are you?'

I thought of Mum and Dad waiting for their drinks, and Sam lying in his high-railed single bed, and I didn't know what else to do. I ran.

Thirty-three

On my way back, I caught Benjy looking through the window of Sam's ward. He rubbed at his eyes with the heels of his hands, wiped them on his black T-shirt.

'Not looking too perky, is he?' he said.

'I'm going to go outside when I've taken these in,' I said, lifting the cardboard cups in my hands. Benjy nodded, and when I walked back out of the waiting room he came with me.

We watched the coloured lines that led to the different areas of the hospital pass beneath our feet. Intensive Care was a peaceful blue. Maternity was black. Benjy stepped over the lines whenever they crossed.

I didn't want to go back in the waiting room. Mum tried too hard to make everyone feel better, and paid too much attention to me. I just wanted her to be quiet and admit she couldn't do anything. I wanted her to leave me alone.

Benjy held the heavy door open for me, and we stepped out into another perfect summer's day. The hospital garden was full of smokers in pyjamas and dressing gowns, some of them laughed in groups and some of them stood alone. One man leaned against his own drip.

'Cancer ward,' Benjy whispered, and when I looked at him he was smiling in his shy way, looking at me with his head tilted away, and I realised how much I'd missed him.

We walked clockwise, breathing in the cafeteria smell of beans and fag smoke and the pollution from the main road, which we couldn't see behind the trees. The grass was scorched and the earth was cracking. Flowers drooped in their beds, some heads so low they kissed the soil.

Benjy stopped at an empty bench and I sat beside him. He set his trainered feet wide, and let out a gigantic sigh.

'Speedboat,' he said, and I looked up at a vapourless aeroplane trailing through the blue, remembering summer days lying with Sam and Benjy and Matty in the paddock.

I picked a daisy and started a game of *He lives, he lives not.*

'Did he tell you about our fight?' Benjy said, and I shook my head. He laughed out of his nose.

'He'd been messing about for ages, climbing out the window when the teacher wasn't looking, nicking food in the cafeteria – and I don't just mean eating potato smileys in the queue, I mean more chocolate than he could fit in his pockets. He loved it. He'd been so good till now, he could get away with anything.

'I thought it was pretty stupid, but it didn't bother me. Free chocolate, so what? But then one day, we were walking out of form room, on our way to RE, and I told him I'd spoken to your mum. It was only us, nobody could hear or anything, and I asked if he was going to blank her forever, just because, I don't even know why, because he's my friend, but he went completely mental.

'He was like, what's it got to do with you, and how dare you speak to her? Like she's not even my godmother any more, and then he went for me. I couldn't believe it! I ran at him and knocked him over. I wish I hadn't – but the girls were all watching by then – I didn't want to fight him. It was stupid. I don't even know how to fight.'

Benjy sniffed and shifted positions.

'Then Hawkins came along and split us up. It was embarrassing. I told Sam not to talk to me, that we weren't friends, and I felt like puking, but he didn't care. The girls were staring at him, and he was sort of peacocking about, like a right dick, all the way to the Head's office . . . I haven't spoken to him since. He was always with that Punky Beresford after that.'

225

Thirty-four

Another night's visiting hours were beginning when our favourite nurse, Mary, with the long dark hair, came out and told us that another ventriculostomy would be performed immediately. We could go in and see Sam before they took him through to the operating room, she said.

'The lorazepam is almost out of his system, so he might be more active than he has been before,' Mary said, and I thought 'active' seemed a strange word to use.

Mum held her hand out as if I was a little girl, and asked if I was sure I wanted to see him. I said of course I was, I'd *already* seen him, more times than she had, and she looked hurt, but I was angry with her for trying to take control suddenly and, more than that, I was disappointed in myself, because part of me didn't want to see him one bit.

Thirty-five

Sam's room was freezing, and he didn't look much like my brother. The skin that wasn't bruised or bandaged was a pale yellow colour. The ventilator sucked and puffed away, and the drip trickled, and Sam rocked his head back and forth on the pillow. His eyes flickered. Mum took one hand, while Dad went round the opposite side and took the other. I stood by Dad, my fingers scuffing Sam's wrist.

Mum talked to him, and he turned his head to her, and away again, and his eyes rolled, right back into his head, so we could see the reds of his bottom eyelids, and he let out this terrible moan, low and brainless-sounding, like a zombie. My fingers flinched away then made their way back, ashamed of themselves.

A terrified look passed between Mum and Dad. I wanted them to put their arms around me.

227

Mary came over. 'Keep going,' she urged. 'He might be able to hear you.'

Mum started again. She told him we were all here, waiting to hear his lovely voice, and not to worry, he was going to be fine, but there was no rush, because we weren't going anywhere – *none of us* – we loved him and we'd wait as long as it took, and the groaning stopped then, and I was so relieved, until he shut his eyes again.

Mary came closer and checked a few things. She told us we were doing great, that it was good to talk to him, that it might be only a matter of time before he woke. She told us how patients waking from comas could be so agitated and confused at first that they tried to leap out of bed or yank their tubes out.

'All excellent,' she said. 'The more frightened they are the better: brain's a-go-go.'

She smiled at each of us encouragingly, and I felt strong and capable, like after a pep talk at half-time.

'Come on, Sam,' I said, leaning over the bed. 'You can do it.'

I grabbed his hand, not caring that Dad's came with it. He was my brother, and whatever Dad thought of me, I wasn't about to let him clear off without a fight.

'Wake up!' I shouted, and Dad shot me a look because there were two other families crowding around relatives in the small Intensive Care room. I saw how

228

his knuckles were yellow, and Sam's fingers purple at the tips from where he squeezed so hard.

Mum smiled at me; a tight, scared little smile.

I shouted again.

And nothing happened.

The noise began, rumbling from somewhere deep inside Sam. It set my nerves on fire. Any hopeful feelings died because it sounded so lifeless, so nothing like him at all.

'You're all right, boy,' Dad tried to soothe, but he sounded heartbroken, like he was telling Sam that he'd love him no matter what.

I felt Mum giving up beside me.

Sam's eyes opened, and he stared straight ahead, and it was like he saw nothing at all.

Thirty-six

Days passed and things didn't get better. On Thursday we were taken into a small room on the seventh floor. There were no windows.

There was me, then Dad, then Mum on padded grey chairs. Mary stood behind us. She had one hand on Mum's shoulder. In front of us was a desk. Leaning against it was one of the consultants: Dr Lloyd. The room was that off-white that schools and offices and doctor's surgeries always are. There were shelves full of textbooks on two of the walls. There were no family photos. It didn't look like anyone in particular's office.

Mary squeezed my shoulder and my stomach dropped. I could hear Mum's breathing, and Dad's. They were breathing too heavily, and too fast.

Dr Lloyd looked from one to the other of them, and occasionally at me, as she talked about Sam. Her grey and white pinstriped skirt was the same colour as her hair.

'Thank you for coming to talk to me today. I won't waste your time. I am terribly sorry to have to tell you that we are going to test your son for brain stem death. The EEG scans were flat. They showed a complete lack of brain activity.'

Dad's head thudded against the wall. He closed his eyes.

Mary stroked Mum's shoulder. The consultant carried on.

'When the brain stem stops working, the brain can't send messages to the body to control even unconscious functions like breathing, blinking, swallowing and coughing. Equally, it can't receive messages back from the body. When this is the case, the person has no chance of recovery. We believe this is the stage your son is at.'

I stared at the rough, lined carpet. At the little balls of fluff.

'I don't understand,' Mum said. 'How can you *know* there is no chance of recovery? How can you be so sure?'

Dr Lloyd explained about the extent of the damage Sam had taken to his head. She talked about the tests they were proposing, but I couldn't follow what she was saying. Something about corneal reflects and gag reflexes. Fixed pupils and water being injected into ears. Mum couldn't follow it either, but she wouldn't stop asking questions.

'I'm so sorry to say this. We believe your son is alive only because the hospital is keeping him that way. The tests have shown no activity in the brain whatsoever after a rapid decline since the seizures.'

Mum talked about miracles. She asked about those stories you hear where people comatose for years wake up and learn to play the piano. She couldn't stop talking. Like maybe if she never stopped, what the consultant was saying could never start being true. Dad stared with closed eyes at the ceiling.

Dr Lloyd told her that these stories were very damaging, that they got people's hopes up unfairly; that they were often propaganda from religious groups.

'Such patients wouldn't be declared brain stem dead in the first place,' she said.

She looked at us, and I hated her for being so unaffected.

'If Sam shows even the *slightest* response to the tests, we will review the whole situation. This is hard for you to accept, but you must prepare yourselves for the worst. We will be very surprised to see a response.'

Mum looked like she might tear Dr Lloyd's face off.

Instead she asked questions. Sometimes she asked

232

the same question again and again. She leaned further and further forward on her chair.

Dr Lloyd glanced at Mary. She gave the tiniest nod.

'The doctors can perform the tests with you present, if it'd help,' Mary said. 'It can help relatives to understand their loved one has really gone. If he has. But it's very traumatic. It can be hard to forget.'

Mum's face lit up at this. She turned in her seat to look at Mary.

'We don't recommend it,' Dr Lloyd added. 'Absolutely not. It is very much the last option.'

Mary bent to talk quietly in Mum's ear about how it was our choice what happened next, but I couldn't hear. Mum was breathing too noisily.

Dad put one arm across each of us as if we were unseatbelted children in a car he was driving too fast.

'No,' he said, very quietly. 'We don't want to see that. None of us will see that. Do the tests.'

Thirty-seven

The three of us sat in the windowless room, in the comfortable chairs, while the tests were carried out. Dr Kang had stayed for a while explaining things to us but I didn't have much idea what she'd said. Apart from that we needed to be prepared for what might happen – but that was impossible.

If Sam didn't respond to any of the tests his support would be withdrawn. If that happened, there would be some time where we could say goodbye before they removed all the breathing tubes and intravenous lines. She told us that we could take as long as we needed, but there wasn't enough time in the world for that.

Shortly afterwards, Sam's heart would stop beating. We could stay with him as he passed away, of course, she said. But that was our decision.

She had asked about the possibility of Sam being a donor – but Mum couldn't take it. She said no, louder and louder, covering her ears like a crazy person. Dr Kang turned her attention to the floor and then told us about the tests.

She and Dr Lloyd would do them together. All of them sounded unbearable, and that was the point. A person shouldn't be able to stand them.

I was worried. If Sam didn't respond and they had to turn the ventilator off, would it feel like choking? Dr Kang said no. She said it wouldn't feel like anything, because if they had to turn the ventilator off, Sam would already be gone. She said he wouldn't suffer, but how did she *know*?

Thirty-eight

Finally, the door opens.

Dr Kang shakes her head. 'I'm so sorry,' she says. 'We did all we could.'

The room shifts and slips and swells.

Objects move around like gravity has been switched off.

Mum is making a loud noise. Her head is between her knees.

Dr Kang is saying we can stay with Sam as he passes, and medicine books are floating through the air like spaceships.

Thirty-nine

The curtains are pulled around Sam's bed. They are pale blue and waterproof and they make a snapping noise when we walk in. He looks peaceful, and it isn't right. Mum goes to him. She says Oh God. She moans No in this terrible low way. She kisses his face. She rests her head on his chest and sobs.

Dad bows his forehead to Sam's. His eyes are squeezed shut. He says My boy, my boy, my boy. No one knows what they are doing.

Sam's hand is warm in mine and I'm not ready to let it go. I want to lie next to him, like we did before, on his bed. I want his hair to grow back, and his dimple to pop and him to call me Eyeball. I don't want to think about what he is, right now, my brother, plugged into machines and breathing and dead.

Mum is hyperventilating. She is clutching at Sam's arms and looking at his face and shaking her head very slowly.

'They can't, they can't, they can't,' she says, she can't stop saying it, and Dad reaches across the bed. He puts his hands on her shoulders.

'He's gone,' he says, and his voice breaks. 'Anna. He's gone.'

Sam's chest rises and falls with the ventilator.

Forty

It's like a black box has opened inside my head. The doctors give Mum something, and Dad buys whisky on the way home, but I'm just here, feeling everything.

Sometimes we're in the kitchen and sometimes we're in Dad's room. Or is it Mum and Dad's room? I don't know, but me and Dad are in our pyjamas. Mum's wearing Sam's navy blue Adidas Stripes and one of his white T-shirts. We don't wash but occasionally Mum makes us all go and clean our teeth. The sun comes up and the moon comes up. And then they go down.

At some point an envelope addressed to me arrives. Inside is something damp and crushed and purple. An iris. It's dead, and sweet-smelling, and I know it means Trick made it home. I put it on my windowsill next to his address. I think about writing to him.

At some point WPC Baker calls round. She wants to know if I'm ready to make a statement. Mum tells her

I'm not. At some point she rings, and Mum says the same thing. Dad doesn't say anything. If I'm near the phone when it rings, and I can get away with it, I hang up without answering.

At some point Father Caffrey comes round. Tess is with him, and an order of service is made. We get old photos out to choose a nice one. Mum has to go upstairs to lie down, so I choose one, from the end of last summer.

Sometimes Tess comes round. She feeds the cats and the dog and puts milk in the fridge. She forgot to stoke the Aga – she didn't know how it worked – and so it's gone out. The kitchen is cold, and full of insects. The windowsills rattle with bluebottles and moths. Daddy-long-legs butt at the strip light.

'Look after your mum and dad,' Tess said to me when we first got back. She had washed all the lasagne plates and was putting a tray of savoury rice in the fridge, and I felt like she was saying I hadn't lost as much as them.

The heatwave continues outside, and the house is getting stuffy when Mum starts asking questions.

'What was he doing out there?' she asks, and it's clear from her voice that her tablets have worn off.

The curtains are drawn and there's a sheet pinned over them. The mirror on the dressing table faces down.

240

Her voice is very flat and very careful, and it makes me sit up because we've covered this; we've been over it a hundred times at the hospital.

Next to me, in the damp bed, Dad takes a swig of whisky. He repeats the sentences that in a certain order explain what happened to Sam.

'But *why* was he out there?' Mum says. 'With those boys. How did he know them? And why was he wearing his football boots?'

She turns to look at Dad, who is the only one still lying down. His neck is tilted against the headboard at an uncomfortable angle. His arm, which must be numb by now, is lodged underneath the pillow I've just moved from.

He lifts himself out of the bed and walks to the window. He pulls the curtains and sheet aside and looks out, rests one fist against the glass. The day shining into the room makes us close our eyes.

'Football boots,' he says very quietly.

'I'm just asking what he was doing out there. How did he meet them? It's a reasonable question.'

Mum continues to list *reasonable questions* in the kind of voice a lioness might discover if it woke one morning on the savannah to find it could speak.

'Bloody good time to come back and take an interest. Bit more of this a few weeks ago and we might have a son we could sit down and give a good talking to.'

241

Mum is standing now. Her cold blue eyes are on fire.

'How *dare* you accuse me of not being interested? I did everything for the lot of you until a few months ago! You didn't know your arse from your elbow! How *dare* you say my leaving was anything to do with my kids!'

They take opposite sides of the room, and I stand between them on the bed. I hold my hands out, telling them to stop. My voice is tinny and unclear. I'm bouncing slightly with the effort of asking them not to fight. I get the urge to laugh.

'*Please*,' Dad says. 'Tell me again why you left. I'd *love* to hear it.'

'I didn't think I loved you any more,' Mum says, and her blue eyes are frightening.

They step closer, until they are shouting into each other's mouths.

'I tell you why Sam was wearing his football boots, Anna. Because I'd hidden all his trainers. Because that's how bad it had got. I didn't know how else to keep him in. I didn't know *what else to do*.'

Mum wants to know why he didn't tell her, why we hadn't let her know.

'Why didn't we let you know? Why didn't we *let you know*?'

Dad's face is purple. He can't breathe.

'Do you remember leaving? Packing a van? Filing for divorce?'

'I would have come back!' Mum shouts. 'I would have *come back*!'

'But *I* didn't know. Don't you get it, woman? *I* didn't know!'

'Why didn't you tell me, Iris?' Mum says 'All those times on the phone. Why didn't you *say* something?'

They are both looking at me now, standing above them as I do, on their bed, swaying slightly, and it's all the wrong way round.

'Nasty habit you've developed,' Dad says, and he's slurring slightly. He stinks of whisky.

'Don't start, Thomas. Please don't start on her.'

'No, don't *you* start. All your love and everybody's equal. Bollocks. You weren't here.'

He points at me, still looking at Mum.

'She left me there, at the hospital, without a flaming clue about what had happened. Looked me in the eye.'

'*Iris!*' Mum calls, but I'm already halfway down the stairs.

All I want is to go outside, to feel the sky above me, to be on my own. Instead I go to my room. I pull Trick's address out from my copy of *The Outsiders*. I copy it neatly, watching my hand as if it's someone else's. I walk back upstairs. It's like looking through the wrong end of binoculars.

243

'What's this?' Dad says, when I hold the address out to him. His voice follows me out the room, terrible and quiet like a balloon full of toxic gas.

'Is this it? Is this his address? How long have you had it?'

I don't stay around for the balloon to explode.

Forty-one

All day I stay out in the corn den. I dig holes in the ditch to go to the toilet. I make a fire and I bake corn. Fiasco chases rabbits, and I will her to catch one so she can eat something and we never have to go home again. Night comes, and I feel like a traitor but all I can think about is Trick.

I keep seeing his odd eyes, the way they looked when Sam was on the floor. I see his chest and stomach, cut up, and his expression, outside my window, when he told me he hadn't wanted any of it.

The further back I go the more it hurts, but I can't stop. I remember him lying next to me in his red vest and jeans, listening to me in that serious way of his. I picture him hiding out here in the dark, his mum and dad shouting, Sam's blood drying on his hands. How much pain he must have been in.

He'll have to go to prison for years. He picked up a

brick and cracked it against someone's skull, and now I don't have a brother.

The stars come out and I stare at them until they throb and grow and shrink again. I remember Sam's face as I washed his cuts at the kitchen table, how he warned me about Trick.

I wish he was here to act smug and rub it in, to say he was right all along. I want to argue it with him, to tell him Trick was backed into a corner, that he should never have started on him in the first place. Suddenly I can hear his voice.

But to brick someone, Eye? That's messed up.

'But Punky cut someone!' I say out loud. 'What's the difference?'

I remember Trick's lip, exploded, his ear ripped at the top where it should join his head, and the bloody tissue in his pocket. I remember Sam's hair, thick with blood, and I regret cuddling Trick, and then I'm back to the unforgettable thing, the thing that is at the beginning and end of every thought, which is that it really doesn't matter if I hugged Trick or not, or if I told Dad about Punky's knife.

Because Sam is never coming back.

I lie in the corn den nestled against Fiasco, not always certain if I'm sleeping or awake, and then I jolt from somewhere warm to heartache, and Fiasco's gone, and Mum is standing over me.

Sun shines through her short hair which is messy in that way that has nothing to do with fashion, and her eyes are swollen and sore-looking. She's wearing Dad's wax jacket over Sam's clothes, even though it's already getting hot.

Fiasco wags her tail treacherously, comes to lick my face.

'Poor old girl must have been hungry,' Mum says. Her voice is empty. 'She been out here with you all night? She ate a whole tin of food just now.'

Mum passes me an apple, and pulls Dad's work flask from her pocket, and sits in Trick's corner. She pours out hot chocolate. I don't know who she is. Her face is so *straight*.

'Got brandy in it,' she says, almost apologetic, and holds the lid out. I take it, amazed at how the milky brown liquid swirls, and how the steam floats up, and how Sam will never again taste a thing as delicious as this.

'We shouldn't have done that. In there. I shouldn't have asked you that. Your dad's right. It wouldn't have made any difference. If you'd told me. If I'd come back. Nobody knew Sam was going to die. How could they? It doesn't make any sense.'

She takes the lid back and refills it, and passes it to me. She swigs from a small bottle of brandy in Dad's pocket. Her whole body trembles.

'He's angry with you now, Iris, but he won't hold it against you. Me, maybe. Not you. He loves you.'

Why isn't he out here then? I want to ask, but my tongue has swollen to the size of an adder. It blocks my throat.

'Loves me too, I suppose.' She shakes her head. 'No suppose about it. He just doesn't always know how . . . He loves you and your brother so much. He cried when you were born. Both of you. Couldn't believe he was lucky enough to get a boy and a girl, in that order.

'He told everyone that's what he wanted, when we were expecting you. "A frilly knicker," he said. I didn't want to curse it, and I didn't mind, as long as you were healthy, but he told everyone, he didn't care. "A frilly knicker, or we're sending it back."'

Mum looks around at nothing, but her voice comes a little bit back to life as she talks.

'All the other men steered clear of the baby phase, but not your dad. He loved it. Nappies, winding, the lot. Let you crawl all over him. Took you everywhere when he wasn't working.'

She looks up. It's another one of those blue and white days. The bright clouds move fast.

'We were happy then, you know. The four of us. I wish you could remember it.'

I drink the last of the chocolate. It's so sweet. The brandy burns my throat. It feels good in my veins.

'You've broken his heart, not telling him things, and he doesn't understand. You're still his little girl. But I . . . It's different with us. All those conversations we had. I know the way you felt about him, Iris. About . . . Trick.'

She swallows in the middle of saying his name, and I want her to stop talking for once because I feel so guilty, but she doesn't. She never does.

'You didn't *do anything wrong*, Iris. Yes, you shouldn't have lied, or snuck out behind his back, but you're thirteen now. Fourteen nearly. He forgets what that's like. He's so old-fashioned! You only did what teenagers do. And this boy. Trick. He was there for you. I know that.'

I wipe my eyes.

'You've got that to deal with on top of everything else, on top of losing your brother. But your dad doesn't think like that. *He knows* you wouldn't lie about what happened, no matter what you thought of this boy. If you held things back . . . He knows you loved your brother. Of course he does.'

I want to talk, to get some of what I'm thinking out, but I'm so scared of saying the wrong thing and, anyway, she won't stop.

'We're so different, me and your dad. Always have been. That's why we liked each other so much at the start. See, I don't care who's responsible. Because nothing can be done about it. It won't stop me feeling guilty and it won't bring Sam back. He isn't coming back. That's all I care about. That's all I've got room for. But your dad, he wants to *do something.*'

'I just feel so sick all the time,' I manage.

'I know you do, baby,' she says, and she pulls me to her.

'No. I mean . . . I feel *so sick.*'

'Look at me, Iris. You've got nothing to feel guilty about. Do you understand? Sam was your brother and Trick was your friend, but what they did had *nothing to do with you.* You don't have to *choose.* Just because me and your dad couldn't live together, didn't mean you had to stop loving one of us, did it? Doesn't work like that. Love doesn't work like that.'

It is like a giant thing has let go from round my neck.

She screws the empty lid back onto the flask, rubs her hands over her face and scratches her head, hard and all over. She strokes her hands across Sam's Adidas Stripes. She looks at me and looks at me and looks at me.

'The only thing we can do now, *the only thing,* is be honest with each other. We have to tell each other how we're feeling, and be honest, and get through this. That's all we can do, Iris. I mean it. That's all we've got.'

She takes my hand, and rubs her thumbs against my fingers, and I dare myself to speak, to say what it is that's making me sick.

'I'm so *angry* with him, Mum, for starting it. He knew Trick was my friend. And he started on him, for nothing. No reason at all. And Trick was scared, Mum. He didn't know what he was doing. They were all on him. He was a mess when I saw him. Afterwards. He was coughing up blood. He waited all night, here, this was our place. His mum and dad left and he waited to see me. To give me his address. And I didn't even know if he'd made it home, but he did.'

Mum is looking at me, chewing her top lip, and I can't carry on. Her blue eyes are wintry.

'It's just so hard to hear, Iris. It's like you're saying . . . It's like you're saying he deserved it.'

'I know,' I say, but I don't stop talking, because she's right. All we can do is tell the truth, and see what's left. 'But if Sam had lived I'd forgive Trick, I know I would, because he didn't want any of it. And what's the difference? Really? He'd still have smashed my brother round the head with a rock. What he did would still be the same.

'It shouldn't have happened, none of it should. But I just can't understand why Sam started on him, Mum. I don't understand why he did it. Why did he do it?'

I don't really know what I'm saying any more, and I feel so far away from things, and then Mum wraps her arms around me.

'I'm so sorry that I left you here by yourself. That

you've been trying to cope with all this . . . You've got to talk to your dad, Iris. You've got to make him see . . .'

She can't talk any more, and it's strange to hear her cry, because all my life I've never seen it, and now she can't stop.

'I thought you'd be all right,' she chokes out. 'I thought you'd all be all right.'

For some reason then, I remember how Sam hated to be laughed at, and all of the times I did it anyway, because I wanted him to feel stupid, and I wonder how anybody can be cruel to someone they love. How can anyone do anything but love each other and be kind when at the end of it all, waiting quietly, sure as the dark at the end of the loveliest day, is only this?

Forty-two

The night before Sam's funeral I slept in his bed. At some point, Dad walked in. He didn't expect me to be there. I could smell the whisky and fags on him. He backed out of the room slowly. I hoped he hadn't thought somehow that Sam had come back.

I have a black linen dress to wear and new black leather ballet shoes. Matty and Donna brought some things round for me to choose from. In the end, they chose for me. I didn't care. Matty tied a black ribbon round my hair, so it was off my face for once.

'You're so pretty,' she said, fiddling with my curls, and I knew she meant she was sorry about everything.

The sun's only just come up, but I put the dress on and sit on my bed. I feel like somebody's sister in a play about a funeral. I wait. Dad gets up too early as well. I can hear him in the shower, and I think about Trick at

253

my window. How Sam opened his eyes in hospital and saw nothing.

On my wall, the girl that is meant to be me stands on a hill before a storm. She looks out at a buzzard that rips a baby rabbit into the sky. The drawing seems threatening now, like a bad omen. I love it. It makes me think of chocolate pancakes. I lie down and pull the covers over my head.

At nine o'clock, Tess and Benjy arrive. Tess has more brandy. She pours three glasses.

Dad isn't down yet. Mum knocks brandy back. She's wearing sunglasses, but no one's mentioned it. Benjy is wearing black trousers and a white shirt, and his hair looks wrong in a side parting.

If it was him who'd died, Sam could have worn his clothes. If it was me, Matty could wear mine. Mum could wear Tess's or the other way round. It's like we're all in costume, and I get the urge to laugh, and then I'm sad because I wish we'd had time to organise something better.

Mum takes her sunglasses off for a second, and her eyeballs are pink. Her eyelids are puffy. She says she's wearing them in the chapel.

'They'll think you're making a statement,' Tess says.

'Screw 'em,' Mum says. 'They make me feel better.'

Tess nods into her glass. She tops Mum up.

254

It's almost time, and Dad still isn't down.

I find him sitting on the end of his bed with his head in his hands. The way he turns his head to me, like a toddler or an animal, makes me run out of the room.

'Mum. You need to go and see Dad.'

She necks her brandy and goes upstairs.

Benjy has been stood by the Aga looking lost. Tess walks over and gives him a cuddle.

Mum's older brothers arrive, Uncle Martin and Uncle Tim, with his wife, Aunty Paula, and my two little cousins. They've been driving since four and the kids are bickering about something. They won't stop. After a few minutes, Tim shouts at them to go outside. They run out, and a minute later we hear them laughing.

Tess asks pointless questions and Uncle Tim looks grateful. Benjy tries to catch my eye.

Mum and Dad come downstairs. He walks through the door first. He's in his funeral suit. He's wearing his thin black tie. Mum's hand is on his back.

She makes a weird noise when she sees her brothers. They hug for a long time.

Unbelievably, though it's what we've been waiting for, the hearse arrives. It's half past nine, time for school assembly, and a stranger in a suit gets out and waits by the glossy black car we'll go in.

255

In the back of the first car is a shiny mahogany coffin that I can't think too much about. It's surrounded by flowers and cards and notes. School held a disco to raise money for a wreath. Sam's nickname, *Dancer*, is spelled out in yellow chrysanthemums. Tess and Benjy and my uncles and aunty look through the windows at the arrangement but me and Mum and Dad just get in the car.

The stranger has teeth like a row of cigarette ends, and when he ducks his head to talk to Mum through the window I can't help staring at them. I can't help wondering what they smell like. The cars pull off, and then we're in the funeral procession.

We sit with our hands on our knees.

A woman with a pushchair stops and bows her head as we pass and I love her.

Inside the funeral car is grey leather. It's a smell you can't forget. On one side, Mum kneads my hand, her rings crushing against the bones of my fingers. On the other, Dad looks like he's going to puke. I want to hold his hand.

The trees kiss overhead, and then we are at the crematorium.

Forty-three

Our car rolls onto the white-stoned car park, and the noise of the tyres is magnified like when Mum left, and I picture Sam running his fingers over the stones, and then the man with the fag-end teeth opens the door for us. Mum climbs out, then me, then Dad, and it's so unusual being at a family event, just us three.

Pretty much everyone I know stands outside the chapel. Matty is on her tiptoes, looking for me. She holds a bunch of white flowers, and her eyes are like Mum's, and I remember how everyone used to tease her about wanting to marry Sam.

Behind her, Donna holds a hanky to her nose. She rests her head against Jacob. They each rest a hand on Matty's shoulders. Austin stands on his own to the side of them. Fraz, Billy Whizz the rabbit catcher, the pig farmer and Big Chapmun stand together, looking itchy in their suits.

Some of Sam's teachers and Miss Ryan, the Head of Year, stand near the back of the group. Most of his form and all his gang are there, as well as some kids from other years. The popular girls, who play netball for the county, clutch at each other as Dad and the other pall-bearers walk over to the hearse. Ally Fletcher who went to the cinema with Sam once starts to cry.

Fraz pats Dad's shoulder, and Benjy's dad, Steve, squeezes Benjy's arm. Mum's brothers Tim and Martin go up together. They all take their places, then pull the coffin out of the hearse, and it's so weird because you can't tell it holds the body of a boy.

He wasn't even sixteen, but his coffin's the same size as a man's would be.

It's not just that he was young, but because it was so sudden. No one should die the way he did: that's what the faces here say.

I think about him, in there, with all that space, and I want to stop them. I want to open the box and climb in with him. I want to wrap him up in a duvet. I can't bear the thought of him being cold.

Father Caffrey comes out of the chapel to meet the coffin. You can see the pall-bearers communicating with each other, very serious and quiet, about when to lift and when to walk. They begin their slow march into the chapel. Benjy's smaller than the rest, but he's in the middle so it doesn't matter. He insisted.

Mum and me follow them in. Her thumb rubbing at my fingers makes my bones ache.

I see Leanne out the corner of my eye as I walk past the crowd. She's sobbing, those gut-wrenching tears I can't do any more. A man with tattooed knuckles wraps his arm around her, looking like he would do anything if she would stop.

There must be a hundred people walking behind us but I don't hear any footsteps. The chapel is cold and it reminds me of Sam's ward. It smells of elderly breath. I want to get out of there.

The intro of 'Tears in Heaven' plays as people file into the pews. Father Caffrey stands at the lectern, serene, nodding at people. The guitar yanks at something deep in me, and for a second I can almost understand what we're all doing here.

The men place the coffin down on the platform at the front left of the chapel, and make their way back to their places. Dad shakes beside me. I hold his hand. It's limp in mine.

Mum sits rigid with her sunglasses on. I can feel her straight spine beside me. Tess is next to her, then Benjy, and then his dad, Steve, on the end.

Father Caffrey lets the guitar fade out. He waits a few seconds to speak. People shift and sniff. The wooden pews creak and the air feels full, because for once everyone is paying attention.

Father Caffrey talks but I don't know what he says. I look at the order of service. Sam's face grins out at me. I took the picture. It's right before school started back last year. Mum's about to tell Sam to calm down because he's just poured a pint of water over Matty while she was sunbathing. Benjy is laughing somewhere out of shot. Sam's hair is really long. It curls onto his forehead, and in front of his ears. You can just see Matty's bare feet in the background.

Tess goes up to read a poem, and it doesn't really matter if it's beautiful or not because I'm holding this picture of Sam, and he looks so delighted, and where is he now? I can't look at the coffin, or at Tess. I keep my eyes on the photo, I don't look away, because it really is getting to be unignorable, the fact that my big brother is dead.

'. . . *nothing now can ever come to any good,*' Tess says, and her voice breaks, and she walks back to her seat. Benjy puts his arm around her.

Father Caffrey invites Mum to the stage, and she stands up, then sits back down. Tess takes hold of her face, and Mum leans in to her. The two of them whisper together, and then Mum shakes her head. She pats Tess's arm, takes a huge breath and walks to the stage. She unfolds a piece of paper, and looks out at the chapel from behind her sunglasses. Tess was right. It does look like a statement. I want her to take them off.

While she scans the first line, Tess slides across the pew, and takes my hand. She drapes her other arm around Benjy. Her fingers are icy and she smells of incense.

Dad is coming back to life beside me. He pulls himself up, and sits tall in his seat, and watches Mum. He squeezes my hand between both of his.

'I don't think anyone can imagine how it feels to be . . . *here*,' Mum says, and there's a strange rhythm to her voice. There are pauses where there shouldn't be. She swallows. She shakes her head from side to side, rubbing her lips over each other. You can just see where her eyes are behind the shades. She looks at me. I want her to sit down.

'The last few days of Sam's life, he was surrounded by his family, and his godmother, and his best friend, and I know that he took comfort from having everyone who loved him most with him, when he breathed his last.'

Dad swallows a strangled sound at this, and Mum looks at the ceiling. We're all remembering the way Sam looked after his ventilator was turned off, how it was like he was gasping, though the doctors said it was only a reflex.

'Our gorgeous son – Samuel Thomas Dancy – named after our fathers, God bless them both, was a funny, talented boy. He was one of the school's best strikers . . .'

'Danc-er!' someone whisper-bellows from the back rows where the school lot are. There is laughing and shushing, and I love whoever it was who dared to do that.

'Dancer,' Mum repeats. She smiles. People shuffle in their pews. 'He loved karaoke – was an even worse hogger than me – and that's saying something.'

Tess lifts her arms up in a silent cheer at this, and Mum nods at her. She is starting to sound a bit like a human.

'And he drew the most beautiful pictures. Put your hand up if you're lucky enough to own one of them.'

Mum puts her hand up slowly, and there is rustling in the chapel as people turn in their seats to see who else has. Me, Dad, Benjy and Tess have our hands up. We can't help but smile at each other.

There's hushed laughter at the back again, and we turn round to see that almost the whole row of girls from the netball team have raised their hands. Some of them are blushing, and some of them are laughing. Ally Fletcher is crying again.

'That's my boy,' Mum says, very softly. She seems to be making it up as she goes along.

'I've often dreamed of Sam's first girlfriend,' she says, and she looks over at where Matty is sitting. I turn to see her beaming back at Mum, wiping her eyes.

'I wondered who would end up being his wife, the mother of his children. I wondered how this girl could

262

ever be good enough for him, and I decided I would treat her as perfect, as long as I could see that she loved him. I always knew Sam would make a good father, because of how he looked out for his little sister, Iris. Because of the father he had.'

Mum looks at me. She bites her top lip. She looks at Dad and they hold each other's gaze for a few seconds.

'Iris worshipped Sam from when she was little. She followed him around as he went on his important adventures, and she would stand up to anyone, however big, if she thought they'd treated her big brother unfairly.'

She goes into the story of me charging at a bigger boy who'd pushed Sam over on the dance floor at a Butlins disco. Dad squeezes my hand. I can't remember it. People laugh.

'The two of them fought like cat and dog, but they never told tales. We could never get out of them who'd started what. And I'm so proud of the way they looked out for each other.'

Mum looks at me for a few seconds, and I think of Sam telling Dad about Trick, the night everything happened, and how it's just something else only Dad and me will know about this summer.

Her voice cracks and she coughs and tries again.

'Sam died too soon. In a way that will make people think of blame and justice. But he was my son. And I choose to focus on the happy times. The fifteen years I had with him were the most beautiful years of my life. Please. Join me in celebrating Sam's life. Remember him as he was. A bossy, happy, funny boy with more energy than he knew what to do with. Talk about him. Remember him.'

Dad has bent his head to my hand, and I can feel his breath and tears prickling on my palms.

Someone claps, and someone else, and the whole room is clapping, and I feel like laughing and crying. I feel euphoric and ecstatic and heartbroken and distraught because Sam's gone, but he was here, and he was amazing, and he was my brother.

Mum comes to sit beside me, and it feels like her skeleton is vibrating when she hugs me.

Father Caffrey invites people to leave things with Sam should they want to. Matty puts an envelope on his coffin, and rushes back to her seat. A couple of the popular girls follow with notes and a teddy, and then the football team place a centre forward bib in school colours next to Sam's picture. I stay where I am. I said everything I wanted when he was alive.

Everyone settles back into their places and the thrashy guitar song Sam tormented us with all summer bangs around the chapel.

The red curtains around the coffin close with an awful whirring sound. I can't look at them. I wish I couldn't hear them. It's a sound you can't forget. I want to get out of the chapel now. Mum and Dad and me leave fast with our heads down.

We stand by the door, at the top of the steps. People slow down to kiss Mum and Dad. They shake their heads and squeeze their hands. They don't know what to say. I wish Mum would take her sunglasses off. She's so stubborn, and then I feel a hand on my back.

'Iris?'

It's Leanne.

She gestures me over to a table a couple of metres away. It is stacked with hymn books and pamphlets.

We need you! a green and gold tapestry shouts above her head.

She scrunches her big mouth over to one side. Her black hair is parted down the middle and her scalp is bluey white. It's the first time I've seen her without her cap on.

'Just wanted to say . . . I'm . . . really sorry.'

'What for? Leaving my brother in the road or punching me in the face?'

Her mouth drops open.

'I'm really sorry. We *had* to go,' she says, and her expression is urgent. 'James and Dean are on probation.'

'I don't care about that.'

265

She seems smaller. She's a different girl. She doesn't know what to say. She just stands there, with her uneven-looking pointy bob, gawping at me.

'Trick stayed,' I say. '*Pikelet*. He stayed with Sam while I went to get an ambulance. So Sam wasn't on his own.'

She looks at her shoes, which are those cheap canvas pumps you have to wear for indoor PE at school. They're rubbing the tops of her bare feet, turning them red.

'He was really special,' she says, and her voice splits. 'He drew me these pictures. I could show you maybe.'

I shake my head.

Matty has come over at some point, and linked my arm, and all of a sudden any anger I had towards Leanne, and even Punky and Dean who haven't even come to the funeral, is gone.

I imagine Sam's drawing version of Leanne – all angular and bright-eyed – and I think of how she cried when he fell, and how she climbed onto the back of the motorbike.

'I won't forget,' I say, and she nods because she won't either, and then she walks off, shoulders low, to find her dad. She buries her head in his chest and he kisses the top of her head.

Matty nudges my arm, but she doesn't hug me. She knows what would happen.

'I made Sam this,' she says, and she holds out a small blue ceramic thing.

I turn it over in my hands. 'What is it?'

'For flowers,' she says. 'It's a vase.'

'Looks like a sock.'

'Piss off,' she says, and she looks so surprised, and then she blows a snot bubble as she laughs or cries or whatever it is we're both doing, and we walk out to the sunshine to see if that feels any better.

Forty-four

Tractors come to harvest the corn.

It is September, and the police have been down to take my statement. It doesn't match Punky and Dean's, but Leanne has told the truth. Trick has told the truth too. I got a letter. He put three kisses, and underlined my name, and there was a drawing underneath which I think was supposed to be an iris. I told Dad what Trick had said, and he nodded. It's still hard to talk about.

My counsellor says I've got to stop going over the order of events. I'm not responsible, he says. There's no point in *What Ifs*.

But what if I can't stop *What If*-ing? I say. He doesn't laugh.

These things take time, he says. He says that a lot.

I'm feeling half sick and half relieved when I hear the tractor engines from the house. I run with Fiasco across the yard, and through the paddock. Dad mowed it finally, and it looks as though nobody has ever been there. We jump across the stepping stones, through the barbed wire, past the ancient oak.

The tractors gnaw along the far end of the field's edges, making their way towards the top of the hill, where our cinema seats are still nailed to that lonely oak tree. I've been waiting for this day. Dad warned me it would be here soon.

I sprint fast as I can, desperate to get there before the farmer sees me. I don't want to talk to anybody. Fiasco runs ahead. As soon as we make it, I wonder if it was a good idea.

Our cushions have been moved around by the weather and are huddled in one corner against the maize, but the stool I nicked from Silverweed squats where it always did. Corn on the cobs rot in a pile nearby, and I think of the iris Trick sent. I hung it up to dry by my window, crushed as it was. The jokers we scrapped from the pack have been blown into the corn.

I pick up the stool and cushions, and lay them in the long grass by the oak tree. I want the tractors to have a clear path.

I help Fiasco to the first fork in the trunk, and climb up myself. I use the nail Trick put in for me.

The tractors close in.

Fiasco scratches at the trunk, panicking at being

so far from the ground. I pat the seat beside me, and she leaps up, bashing her tail against the burgundy velvet.

The noise hurts my ears. When I part the branches, one of the tractors is coming straight for the corn den. The ground shakes. The tree judders. It passes right by us, hacking at the stalks to get the crop. Fiasco jumps onto my lap and I hug her.

'Don't worry, girl. There's nothing to be frightened about. I'll look after you. It'll be okay.'

I stroke her long brown ears, and she calms down.

I think of Trick, in his red vest and rolled-up jeans, smelling of cigarettes though I never saw him smoke one.

I think of his odd eyes, and how nice he'd looked when he'd sat on the caravan steps holding something in his hands with his little sisters crowding round. I remember the way he used to look at me, as if I was weird and special and lovely, and what it felt like when we kissed on the lake.

I remember lying on the bed with my warm brother. I remember chocolate on his chin. The way his dimple popped. I remember listening to stories in his bedroom, before it all happened. There was nothing I wished I'd said to him. There was nothing I wished I hadn't said.

*   *   *

The tractors have long finished when I climb down. It's that part of the day when shadows are long and the air is golden. I hold my arms out, and after a lot of encouragement, Fiasco jumps into them.

With the corn gone, you can see for miles. All the way to Ashbourne Road. The fields around me are empty except for miles and miles of yellow stubble. It's a different place.

The sky is cloud-free and blameless, and the sun is sinking down after the first autumn day of the year. Overhead a single vapour trail soars upwards.

The summer is over, but it will always be my brother's season.

I imagine that every year he will come to see me, when the shadows are long, and the sun is coming down like this, and the world is showing how beautiful it is possible for things to be.

Soon I will be older than him, but I'll chase him anyway, like a little sister, and always he'll be running just along at the edges of things, and always he'll be turning a corner, just ahead.

Liquorice Cigarettes

A prequel scene
by C.J. Flood

Safia was Mum's most glamorous friend, or that's what Mum always said. Apparently we'd met her, but I didn't remember. She wasn't much more than a voice on the phone and a name on one of my birthday cards. She'd moved to Tunisia when I was five, and if me or Sam left wet towels on the bathroom floor, or tomato sauce on the plates we were supposed to have washed up, Mum threatened to go and live with her.

It was a standing joke, or so we thought, and then last Easter, on Mum's birthday, when things were bad, she went for a visit.

'I'll be nicer when I've had a rest,' she told Sam and me. 'You'll have a much better time with your dad.'

She was right.

That weekend, Dad let me and Sam build a zip wire in the yard, and we invited our mates round to whizz down it. In the evenings, his friends came over with sausages and burgers to barbecue. They took beers from a barrel of iced water until there were none left, and Sam and I dared each other to nick cans of Skol and Marlborough cigarettes when they weren't looking. We shared them round the back of the house, eating hotdogs and watching meteors streak the sky.

Dad didn't even complain when Mum asked to extend her stay.

She rang every other night, and Sam spent ages asking about Beni Khiar, where Safia lived, and telling her what we'd been up to, but when it was my turn, I couldn't think of anything to say. I told her I missed her, and that Maud, our cat, was pregnant, and that the house felt empty with her gone, but only the thing about the cat was true, and when she returned, two weeks later, I could hardly look at her because I felt so guilty.

Her first day back, she made one of her fancy dinners, with candles and everything, but instead of a starter, a main and a pudding, she loaded the table with the wonky bowls she'd brought back with her. They were full of different stuff. The kitchen smelled of lemons and cinnamon and garlic as Sam and me sat down, and Mum fussed around us, talking all the time. Dad took his seat, with his blank face on, as if nothing was different. As if we always sat down to eat like this.

Mum explained what everything was, and how cheap the bowls were, and how important it was to haggle over there. She loaded up each of our plates as she talked, putting the most on Dad's because he'd been working all day. He hadn't had a shower even though he'd been back for a while, and there was dirt in the creases of his forehead, but Mum didn't tell him off.

'There's a real art to it,' she said. 'You'd have loved it, Sam. I kept wishing you were there with me to get me a better deal. And, oh my goodness, the girls are *stunning*.'

Mum spooned vegetable couscous onto our plates.

'What about the boys?' I asked, trying to join in.

'Oh, the boys!' she exclaimed. 'You should see their *eyes*, Iris. All melty and brown and lovely-looking. One time at the souks – that's what they call the markets over there—'

'What is that?' Dad interrupted, pointing at the small bowl of thin red sauce Mum was spooning onto our plates.

'Harissa, a sort of chili thing.'

'Be too bloody hot for me, won't it?' Dad said, and he sounded annoyed that something he couldn't eat had even made it onto the table.

'Why don't you just try it?' Mum said, spooning a tiny bit onto his plate, and her voice was too exasperated, as if Dad had said he couldn't possibly eat any of it, and had got up from the table and walked out.

Sam shoved food into his face, oblivious, and I wondered why he never seemed to notice these things.

'What about the souks?' he said, before ramming a forkful of couscous into his mouth.

'Well! One time, Safia and I ran into this boy – not much older than you, Iris – we literally ran into him! We were on our way—'

Dad's chair screeched across the kitchen floor suddenly. He went over to the sink, and put his head down to the tap.

'Bloody hell!' he said.

Mum looked over at him, blankly. 'Don't be melodramatic, Tom. Eat some couscous. Water'll make it worse. You need carbohydrate to soak it up...'

Dad wasn't listening. He grabbed with his mouth at the cold water, which was running so fast that it sprayed out of the sink.

'You'll make it worse,' she chided.

'It's not even that hot,' Sam said, but I'd seen him knock back his water ages ago, and there was still a red patch on his plate.

'It's how they eat things over there,' Mum said, helping herself to more. 'Must've got used to it. Sorry.' She shrugged.

Dad turned the tap off, and the kitchen was silent except for mouths chewing and cutlery scraping.

'Iris! I forgot to give you these!' Mum said. 'Have you tried them before?'

I shook my head, and she dropped three tiny silver fish onto my plate.

'Anchovies,' she said, as if she'd magicked them up herself, rather than bought them from the fish market on Friargate.

Dad took a clean tea towel from the drawer, and wiped his face roughly, sniffing.

'In Tunisia,' Mum announced, 'there's an old wives' tale that says a husband can judge his wife's affection by the amount of hot peppers she uses when preparing his food. If the food becomes bland, then a man may believe his wife no longer loves him...'

I trawled through my dinner without an appetite. Sam reached for more couscous.

'We're not in Tunisia though, are we, Anna?' Dad said.

'No,' Mum said. 'We're not.'

She loaded more food onto her fork.

Standing in the middle of the kitchen, Dad stared at her, but she didn't look up. There was a ragged wet line across his t-shirt from where water had splashed out of the sink, and his eyelashes were clumped together.

'And that's supposed to mean something, is it?' he asked, loudly.

Sam looked up. There was a spot of olive oil on his chin. He was chewing with his mouth open, and Mum didn't tell him off.

'Not at all,' she said very politely, like she was talking to a teacher on parents' evening. She turned a piece of roasted courgette red with harissa, and put it into her mouth.

Dad watched her. I could hear him breathing through his nose, and all the things I'd eaten lay heavy in my stomach.

I wanted to give him a cuddle, and tell him I'd left mine too, that it *was* hot, but I stayed quiet. I didn't want to make things worse. She'd only just come back.

Finally, he unhooked his leather jacket from the back of the door.

'What about your dinner?' Mum said. 'You're just going to leave it now? I spent a long time making that, Tom.'

'I'll get something at The Stag,' he said, and he stalked out of the kitchen. A minute later, we heard the pick-up pull off.

Mum's head dipped at the sound of that, and she stared at her fork for longer than was necessary considering it wasn't doing anything at all. She was always telling him not to drive if he was going to have a drink. Shaking her head as if to clear it, she took a deep breath, and then a swig of wine, and then she started talking again, about Tunisia, and all the adventures she'd had, and how next time she'd take us with her.

When we'd finished, she cleared the table with just a little bit more force than was required in every movement.

Sam went upstairs to finish a drawing he was working on for Ally Fletcher who he was building up to asking out.

When I'd dried all the pots, and Mum had wiped down the sides, she asked if I wanted to do some guitar practise, and we went up to the spare room. We called it the spare room, but it was Mum's room really, full of her music books, and guitars and cactuses. There was a sofa bed too, which she slept on more often than we were supposed to notice.

I strummed clumsily because that was all I could manage, and she picked, but instead of the sad combinations of chords she usually called out, she got us making a happy sound.

After a while, her frown lines were almost completely relaxed. She put down her guitar, and looked at me in a way that was confusing. Her long hair had got lighter from the sun and her freckles were out.

'Did you have a nice couple of weeks?' she said, tucking her hair behind her ears, and I shrugged, fingers still hovering hopefully over the frets, wanting to escape scrutiny.

'Sam sounds like he did,' she said. 'He said your dad had his mates over a lot, that you barbecued.'

I tapped the frets, listening to the reverb.

'D'you think your dad had a nice time?' she said, and I didn't know what the right answer was. I started playing the guitar like it was electric, sliding my fingers along the strings so that they screeched. Mum tilted her head at me, and blinked, and I felt like a specimen.

'Do I seem different, Iris?' she asked.

Her hands were relaxed at her sides, and her burgundy nail varnish was chipped, and she wore no make-up. Without it I could see her real face, the one she usually coloured over, first thing in the morning, and I could see how, alone, her features were ordinary, but together they added up to something beautiful.

'You've got a tan,' I said, and she laughed, and rested her guitar against the book shelf.

'I feel so calm,' she said, stretching her legs out. 'Not angry at all. Not even after...' she trailed off, and my stomach did a back-flip. 'I just feel so... *happy*,' she said, and her face broke into a grin. I smiled back at her, but I felt sick.

She pulled me into a cuddle, and rubbed at my shoulders roughly, in this way of hers that she said got the cirulation going, and I wondered what my face had done to tell her I was upset, and if I would ever learn how to stop it from doing that.

'Don't you want me to be happy?' she said, after a while, and I felt like crying, but in her smell of sweat and apples and the liquorice cigarettes she'd brought back from the souks, I must have nodded, because she said, 'I know you do, baby. I know you do,' and she rocked me back and forth.

Acknowledgements

First acknowledgements must go to my mum and dad, for their endless support and general magnificence. To Liam, because he is the reason I so love to write about big brothers. And to Josie Richmond and all of my extended family, for their support.

So many people have helped this book along the way, and I would like to thank:

All my workshop friends at the University of East Anglia, especially Anna Delany and Tim Cockburn, and Andrew Cowan who believed in this book early on. Nicola Barr, who gave excellent feedback as my agent mentor, and The Lucky 13s for all their energy, enthusiasm and wisdom.

Bernardine Evaristo for being an inspirational mentor, and everyone else who helped make the Jerwood/Arvon Mentoring Scheme so wonderful. The Curtis Brown Agency, Grants for the Arts, and Norwich

Writers Centre, for making the finishing of this thing much, much quicker.

Max Naylor, who had to read my earliest attempts at writing, and Fiddy Matthews, Ursula Freeman, Molly Naylor, Em Prové and Clare Howdle, who are my heroes.

Everyone at Simon and Schuster for all the work they have done for this book. Phil Earle, who helped with the title, Frances Castle and Nick Stearn who have made it look so very beautiful, and especially Venetia Gosling who pushed me to work just a little harder with every passing edit: I hope the words do the cover justice.

Finally, Catherine Clarke for believing in my writing and getting people to read it, and for helping it to meet the world in the best shape it could be.

Thank you.
C.F.

282